A Seat in the Circle

To my wife Morag

© Bill Montgomery

Published 1998 by
The Bluecoat Press
Liverpool

Book design by
March Design

Front cover illustration by
Peter Whitfield

Printed by
Gardner & Company (Liverpool)

All rights reserved. No part of this publication may be reproduced, stored in a retrieval system, or transmitted in any form or by any means, electronic, mechanical, photocopying, recording or otherwise, without prior permission from the publisher.

ISBN 1 872568 52 1

A Seat in the Circle

Bill Montgomery

The Bluecoat Press

Foreword

A few years ago, when BBC Radio Merseyside asked me to produce the *Weekend Inn* programmes for Saturday and Sunday evenings, I was looking for some means of featuring a different 'show-biz' personality each week and of presenting the item to the listeners in a fresh and interesting manner. In particular, I was thinking of those legendary film stars who we all went to see on the 'pictures' before the days of the 'movies' arrived.

I duly devolved the task to our general, Bill Montgomery, who was a film buff of many years standing. He must have known his stuff sitting down as well, because he came up with the superb idea of the weekly feature, *A Seat in the Circle.* And how popular it became! I can hear it now! As the sound of the musical fanfare faded away, we were held spellbound as the scene was set, the atmosphere created and the story commenced.

But who were we hearing about this week? We didn't know at this point! We had to keep listening intently to become aware of who the featured personality was, as their identity was cleverly woven into the narrative. Then followed all those points of interest not known to us before. Fascinating!

We were hooked! And still are! So here they are folks, in print for the first time! Tales that are happy, sad, haunting and sometimes shocking but all interesting and very well written. If you haven't heard them before, you're in for a treat. If you have, you can relive again those few minutes each week when you first heard these tales about the not so public side of famous people's lives. So, are you ready? Action! Camera! Cue the music! Ladies and gentlemen take your places for *A Seat in the Circle.*

Billy Maher BBC Radio Merseyside

Roy Castle

When Bill Montgomery asked me if I would write a few words for his book, I felt quite proud! When he told me he was donating the proceeds to Roy's Appeal, I felt quite moved.

As a lung cancer sufferer, I more than most know the true worth of a donation such as this and the good it will achieve in alleviating this scourge of our society.

Roy's courageous fight against his illness left its mark on everyone. His determination inspired people everywhere to help realise his dream. I doubt if there is another city anywhere, where the people would have taken a cause to their hearts like they have done here in Liverpool. The legacy Roy has left in the Research Centre will one day ensure that countless generations of the yet unborn will never know the horrors of this dreadful disease and the words lung cancer will be consigned to the history books where they belong.

Terry Kavanagh

A Seat in the Circle

Thank you for purchasing this copy of *A Seat in the Circle*. I have had great pleasure in compiling the stories from the facts of stage and screen. I am also pleased to donate the proceeds of this book for the benefit of the Roy Castle Appeal.

In 1991, I joined Sunshine Hospital Radio, which broadcasts to Fazakerley and Walton Hospitals. As a retired financial consultant, I could devote time to help patients by making their stay a bit more comfortable. Way back in the Sixties, I was a long-term patient, spending some of my convalescent time playing patient's requests on a small record deck. Ken Dodd presented his hit single, *Love is like a Violin*, to add to our small collection. Believe it or not, it is still there!

Sunshine Radio is now in its twentieth year and six years ago gave me the opportunity to broadcast a programme, which had a slant on the movies. The stories and the music had been subjects of great interest to me since I was a small boy attending the Majestic (Daulby Street) and the Kings (London Road) cinemas with my mother. How ironic that the Roy Castle Research Centre has been erected between the sites where these two cinemas stood.

My interest in the movies brought me guest spots on local radio with presenters Billy Butler, Wally Scott, Clive Garner and Billy Maher. The foreword, kindly penned by Billy Maher, will give you extra insight as to how it all started and the two years of *A Seat in the Circle* which drew up to one hundred letters a week, from Cheltenham to Stranraer. It is the listeners of Radio Merseyside who have requested that I put *A Seat in the Circle* down on paper so that it can be enjoyed in their armchairs!

Thank you for supporting our venture and I hope you enjoy it!

Mention **Fatty Arbuckle** today and most people think of the restaurant on the Edge Lane complex that is named after this great artiste of the 1920s and proudly displays memorabilia of his era. He was the highest paid star of his time and laid the path for other comics to follow. Even our own Charlie Chaplin was inspired by the comic genius to take the long trip to America to join the talents of Buster Keaton, hoping that they would become as big as the American star, in fame if not in stature.

Roscoe Arbuckle arrived in Hollywood from vaudeville in 1909. By 1913 he was the leading star for the Max Stennett studios, Keystone, famous for its *Keystone Cops*. Max Stennett was now turning out two hit series, the Cops and the Fatty films. Arbuckle made dozens of hit movies. In 1917, he decided to form his own film corporation, directing most of his films which included the young Buster Keaton. The Corporation was making a lot of money and Arbuckle was worth his weight in gold. He could do no wrong. Everybody wanted to know him. If Fatty wasn't throwing a party, someone else was and Fatty was invited. Some of these parties had the reputation of wild living but those attending considered them just clean fun. There were always plenty of girls, outnumbering the males by three to one and some of the parties carried on for a couple of days. Money was plentiful and the champagne flowed. The young starlets were trying to break into films, dressed in scanty dresses and saying and doing all the right things. Some made it to the top. Those who did not stayed mostly on their backs, ending up in escort agencies which provided the wild-living parties with batches of girls, sometimes fifty at a time. Fatty Arbuckle was continuously merry-making, seven days a week, as were many of the other stars but Fatty had a bigger reputation as a raver because he stood out in a crowd.

On Labour Day in 1921, Lionel Sherwell and Freddie Fubach, two big names of the 1920's movie-world, invited Fatty Arbuckle to a big celebration party in San Francisco. A model by the name of Virginia Rappe caught the attention of Fatty Arbuckle and they disappeared into one of the many rooms of the mansion. An hour later Fatty informed the party hosts that Virginia needed a hospital. Virginia was dead. The police were called in after a doctor's examination. The result of the hospital's investigation was that Virginia had been raped. An internal examination after Virginia's death revealed that her cervix had been ruptured by a large instrument, although the nature of what this had been was not known. The only clue was that there has been plenty of champagne for the celebrations.

Fatty Arbuckle was tried for manslaughter. When the first jury could not reach a verdict, a new trial brought the same conclusion. At a third trial, Fatty was acquitted but those who were once his friends turned against him. He lost his corporation as his fortune dwindled because of the costs of his defences. The big movie bosses barred him from making any more movies and independent cinemas were blacklisted if they ever showed his films. His life was wrecked, he was a destroyed man.

Buster Keaton, one friend who had cushioned a lot of the blows, stood by him and, after some years, allowed Fatty to direct some of his films, bringing him back from obscurity although he suggested that Fatty change his name to William B Goode, and also William Goodridge. Using these aliases, he successfully directed other famous stars such as Eddie Cantor and Marion Davis. Fatty Arbuckle died in 1933, a forgotten man.

So, if you ever go to Fatty Arbuckle's restaurant to celebrate, take a tip from me – don't order the champagne!

The street lighting reflects on the wet pavement in London's Leicester Square. The crowds take up every available position to view the Queen and the stars who are congregating for the Royal Premiere film at the Odeon cinema. The rain is still falling as the stars begin to arrive under many colourful umbrellas. The canopy shelters the stars as they step from their Rolls Royces. Photographers' flash bulbs pop and the crowds scream with delight as Bridget Bardot stretches a shapely leg from her limousine. Her high heel creates a ripple in a puddle of water, making the lamplight waver in the reflection. Robert Mitchum causes a stir and the screams reach a deafening crescendo in the damp night air. Some of the girls break ranks as they try to touch their hero. After an hour of more screams and flash bulbs, the stars are in their seats awaiting the Queen, who arrives to be welcomed by Lew Grade and some of the big movie producers from around the world. The foyer is alive with technicians from the newsreels, making the atmosphere electric.

One person standing at the entrance is a tall member of the Odeon staff. He is a very important figure to the movie fan – yes, the doorman who is dressed in immaculate regalia. His good looks are enhanced by a dimpled chin, similar to that of Kirk Douglas. One of the top producers standing near him weighs him up and thinks that this good looking guy has star potential. What was he doing keeping door for a cinema chain?

"Hello," said the producer, "I'm Les Steinster, here's my card, give me a call tomorrow."

The doorman arrives at the block of offices the next day and makes his way to the plush office on the fourth floor. The receptionist comes to his aid.

"Can I help you?" she asks.

"Errr ... yes," the doorman replies in an Irish brogue. "I was asked by Mr Steinster to call. Here is his card. My name is William Miller."

Bill Miller takes a seat in a well upholstered chair, finding it rather difficult not to fall asleep. The secretary returns.

"Help yourself to coffee, Mr Miller. Mr Steinster is tied up in a meeting right now. In the meantime, would you like to fill in this form, just for the records? We would like to know a bit about you. It is self explanatory."

Bill studies the form, deep in thought while sipping his drink. He then reaches for his pen to give a rough outline of his past life.

"I was born on 4 July 1928, in Belfast. My good looks always brought comments from my friends that I should be in films. After an ordinary upbringing, I decided to try my luck in Canada in 1946. As there is a large Irish contingent there, as well as some of my friends, I thought it would possibly be a stepping stone to fame. I decided to get myself noticed. I had a good physique and training developed it to the full. Running around the local parks soon got me in with the acting fraternity and I was known as a keep fit fanatic. Next came radio and I was fairly popular on the Canadian air waves. The amateur repertory companies gave me the opportunity to shine. So radio and stage kept me going for four years but there was never that man in the audience to say that I should be in films. I returned home before taking my chance in England. My fanatical keep fit programme was still on the agenda, in between finding work in cafes and hotels, and on to my present employment of doorman at the Odeon, Leicester Square, in the West End of London."

The receptionist returns. "Mr Steinster will be with you now, Mr Miller, would you go through to his office and take a seat."

"Well, Mr Miller" says Les Steiner, "how nice of you to come, sorry for the delay. I would like some tests at the studio tomorrow if that's alright with you?"

"Fine by me" replies Bill.

"About your name, William Miller," says Les, scratching his chin, "No! I think we will give you a more of a cowboy name like Boyd, but we can't call you Bill Boyd because he is Hopalong Cassidy. I know, what about Stephen Boyd?"

So the ex-Odeon doorman breaks into films in 1955. His dimpled chin soon make him a favourite with the film-goers. His first film *An Alligator Named Daisy* does not set the world on fire. But films like *The Fall of the Roman Empire, Ben Hur, The Bible, Fantastic Journey* and one of my favourites, *The Man Who Never Was*, bring him international fame. The fitness centres wherever he films could always be sure of the presence of Stephen Boyd. His remarkable fitness and talent always keep him in with the in-crowd. If he isn't on the running track or lifting weights, he is relaxing on the golf course.

In 1977, while near to finishing the film *The Squeeze*, a game of golf is in progress after another keep fit session. While Stephen is making a long drive, he collapses from a heart attack. He is only forty nine but his fanatical fitness regime has proved just too much for the human body.

The young French actor was roused from a deep sleep to be told that he had twelve hours in which to learn the script of the leading role in a play which was about to open in Paris. The leading actor had fallen ill; the producer was about to cancel the production until someone else could be found and this would need at least another fortnight of rehearsals. Cancelling the production appeared the most logical step to take. The director had taken the leading man to hospital after he had collapsed on the final day of rehearsal. While on the return journey to the theatre, his thoughts were on a replacement and who would be available in two weeks time. He thought of the young actor who had arrived in Paris a year earlier who had an exceptional memory for learning lines. He could speak German, Italian, Portuguese and Spanish. He was only twenty years old and had graduated from the acting academy within twelve months of arriving from the town of Figeac, South West France, where he was born in 1899. He was exceptionally handsome and had a fascination for the theatre and films.

"Charles, are you awake … wake up at once." The landlady shakes the shoulder of sleepy-eyed Charles Boyer. "You must go to the theatre at once. It is urgent." Charles rubs his eyes.

"What's all the fuss, I don't have to be at the theatre till tonight and I only have a small part in the play?" he mumbles.

"It is urgent" insists his landlady, "You must go now!"

Charles Boyer gave an exceptional performance to a delighted audience and became an overnight celebrity. He learned the script within twelve hours without rehearsing with his fellow actors. Within the next four years, he was toasted as the crown prince of the theatre by Henry Bernstein, a dominant theatre figure. Hollywood was now calling but, despite all his linguistic talents, he could not speak English. It was 1927 and the year of *The Jazz Singer* and the talkies. MGM offered Charles a contract for their foreign films but he was not happy and a German film company invited him to work. Hollywood coaxed him once again as his English was improving and he could make himself understood, but it took some time for his career to get off the ground. He was always invited to the many film functions and it was at such a party, after the completion of the film *David Harum*, that he noticed an up-and-coming starlet by the name of Pat Patterson. He couldn't take his eyes off her. To coin an old phrase – it was love at first sight.

They were complete opposites in both temperament and personality. She was a lively, pretty blonde with a bubbly nature. who loved making films and the money and life style that went with them. Charles was good-looking but very serious and dedicated to perfecting his acting. Nevertheless, their love for each other was there for all to see. Pat was born in Bradford and appeared in many London musicals and British films before Twentieth Century Fox captured her for the Hollywood musicals which were all the go in the 1930s.

Charles and Pat tried to be with one another as much as possible. They were completely devoted to each other's success. Charles' career was taking off and Pat, though successful in her own right, started to take a back seat to push Charles forward to stardom. This he achieved and became the heart-throb of the Thirties and Forties. By 1945, he was the highest paid star at Warner Brothers and the best known screen lover since Rudolph Valentino. He was matched with the most beautiful stars in the most passionate love stories and he performed with as much vigour as you were allowed to in those movie-mad days.

His leading ladies included Claudette Colbert, Marlene Dietrich, Bette Davies, Olivia de Havilland, Rita Hayworth, Ingrid Bergman and Lauren Bacall to name but a few. All his films had classic story lines and not many dry eyes. Filming with all those beauties presented no temptation for Charles. Even though there was many a temptress who wanted to conquer the world's greatest lover, after a day's filming Charles only wanted his Patricia.

The press could not find even a slightly murky story against this devoted man. At the end of a film, the love birds were never out of each other's sight. The press described their marriage as sheer magic. While most of their film and celebrity friends were getting divorced, their love became stronger and stronger. Their marriage appeared complete when their son, Michael, was born.

Charles could have made more movies than he did but chose to be with his wife. He made shrewd investments in television companies which boosted the Boyers' millions. For thirty years, life for the Boyers was wonderful, then tragedy struck –- Michael was found shot dead. This was a great blow to the couple and they never fully recovered, only managing to hold on because of their devotion to each other. They sold all the homes that had any connection with Michael as they could not bear the pain of any memories.

In 1977, Charles was not feeling too well and was advised to go to New York for a specialist examination. After the results had shown that there was nothing to worry about (in fact he was given a clean bill of health) they held each other in their arms, holding back tears of anxiety. They still had one another. Charles suggested that Pat have a thorough examination while they were there. After the examination the doctor broke the bad news to Charles. Pat had incurable cancer and only had one year left to live. Their world was coming to an end. He comforted her during those next twelve months, his heart broken. He held her in his arms every night till they awoke in the morning. Then one morning Pat did not awake – she had died in her sleep. As you can appreciate, Charles was devastated.

Charles Boyer committed suicide in order to be buried with his beloved Pat in Holy Cross cemetery, Los Angeles. Many of his films ended with his fans reaching for their handkerchiefs. This time, it was the end of Hollywood's greatest love story.

It is four o'clock on a Sunday afternoon in the early Fifties. The queue for the circle stretches for two hundred yards down Daulby Street, turning up Oakes Street for another three hundred yards, until it reaches the timber-yard at the back of the cinema. The end of the queue has now collided with the back end of the stalls queue which stretches four hundred yards along Pembroke Place to the entrance. There is no way that all these picture-goers are going to get in the first house, the tail-enders will be lucky to get into the second. The Majestic is the most popular cinema locally, seating eighteen hundred. With nearly four thousand in the queue, the buskers were in heaven. The little man with the zither plays the three tunes that make up the whole of his repertoire before thrusting his old battered hat into the queue. The end of his third tune gave him the nickname Harry Lime because that was the theme he played. What other cinema could boast of a queue of four thousand? It was more like a queue for tickets for a football game.

The ever popular Majestic was built in 1937, replacing the old Majestic which had been built in 1914. The New Majestic's illuminated front tower was an impressive seventy five-feet tall. It opened with *Waikiki Wedding*, starring Bing Crosby. Standing on the fringe of town with a local population of nearly forty thousand gave the cinema a head start. The population dwindled when houses were demolished to make way for a new hospital, starting the decline of London Road. That corner of Daulby Street, Pembroke Place and London Road brought happiness to thousands of Liverpudlians till the day the Majestic closed with Alfred Hitchcock's film *The Birds* in 1970.

Twenty five years later, a new building is being constructed, a special building which many thousands have contributed towards in the memory of a very brave man who showed enormous courage and humour through great suffering. The Centre of Excellence for Research into Lung Cancer will throw a shadow over the former site of that Majestic cinema. Majestic – a fitting word for the man that this new structure honours and commemorates. God Bless you, Roy Castle!

T'**wo young boys,** from different parts of the country, joined the best touring group of the day, Fred Carno's 'Casey's Court'. This was the foundation which brought out the talent you would need to succeed in Variety. They both learned their craft and each became very funny in their own right. By now, they were both seventeen and ready for the outside world. Dave, from Liverpool, whose special talents were his quick silvered wit and his funny stories, was very different from his mate, whose talents lay in his antics and his ability to make audiences laugh without saying a word. The two comedians were so different that they could never have formed a duo. It was time for the two comics to move on and say goodbye to Fred Carno, the man who had made hundreds of Variety stars.

Dave stuck to his roots and appeared at all the best local Variety halls including the Olympia, the Royal Hippodrome and the Empire. You did not have to travel very far in those days as Variety was the in-thing and the rewards were substantial. Dave stayed because of his relatives, no fewer than eight of whom also performed in Variety.

Charlie's ambition was to conquer America and the teenager set out to do just that. Everywhere he went, he auditioned, clowning about, waiting for someone to discover him, until Max Stennett of Keystone Cops fame sat up and took notice of the artistry of this funny little man with the bowler hat, bent cane and moustache. Yes, Charlie Chaplin had arrived and he went on to become the king of comedy. He was loved all over the world because the silent screen meant that there were no language barriers. He was a perfectionist and because of this he went on to direct his own films. Later, he produced them, buying and building his own studios. Charlie carried on making silent films long after the talkies had arrived because he felt that the comedy element would be lost in sound. He always had his critics and, like many Hollywood greats, was branded with the communist slur that eventually drove him out of America. But Charlie had plenty of qualities and he developed into writing brilliant musical scores for his films. This was noted by music lovers worldwide when he produced the score of the beautiful *Limelight*. This haunting melody was on everyone's lips and it may never have been written had the great Chaplin not been forced from America. It remains one of the light music classics – when one hears the refrains of *Limelight* one thinks of Chaplin.

Dave, his mate who stuck to his Liverpool roots, was a success in his chosen direction but was never in Chaplin's class. He carried on entertaining throughout Merseyside up to the point when his act needing updating. Many of the halls were changing due to the popularity of cinema and started showing films as well as Variety acts. This, of course, cut down on the bookings, leaving the minor artistes out of work. As bookings became scarce, the semi-professional was born. The smaller halls then went completely over to the cinema, leaving only the big theatres with the monopoly of the first class entertainers. Age and change forced Dave to take the avenue of the semi-professional and it was not too long before the Variety stage was a thing of the past for him. He moved into administration with the Liverpool Warehousing Company and for many years he entertained the staff with his memories of Variety.

What might have been if he had gone the six thousand miles with Charlie? The ex-comic would reminisce to his nephew, enthralling him with stage stories, making the boy stage-struck. His uncle helped his small hands turn over the heavy pages of the giant scrap books that contained large, black and white photos of Dave standing next to the great Charlie Chaplin in scenes from Carno's 'Casey's Court' and casual pictures of them taken as mates. Dave's nephew was so proud of his uncle. His arms were tired as he got to the fourth scrap book with photographs of some of his other uncles and aunties appearing in their Variety regalia. Eight of these photographs, were displayed in the shop window next to the Royal Hippodrome when it celebrated its centenary. Dave's family had certainly played their part in the city's rich history of entertainment.

Dave's ill health brought full-time employment to an end but he was still fit enough to cling on to a bit of nostalgia by being night caretaker at the Royal Hippodrome cinema on West Derby Road, Liverpool; a theatre in which he had appeared on many occasions before audiences of almost three thousand. But the theatre is empty as he moves his old body from the wings at the side of the massive safety curtain towards the centre of the stage. The house lights have been turned up. From the centre of the stage he gazes into the vast auditorium. The empty seats bring a tear to his eye and a lump comes to his throat as he reaches for his handkerchief. He moves wearily back to the wings and dims the lights. The dressing rooms seem to cry out that familiar sound – "Five minutes on stage, Dave." The old entertainer carried on loving the nostalgia at the famous theatre right up until he died.

The once small boy was proud of his uncle. He also loved Charlie Chaplin. But the limelight shone only on his uncle Dave.

This story is true … I was that little boy!

It is 1922 and the crowd is pouring out of the Adelphi Theatre on Up Broadway. Up Broadway means that the theatre had a capacity of more than four hundred seats, less than four hundred was Down Broadway. There is no top or bottom to Broadway as it is just an area like London's West End. Right bang in the centre of this metropolis of night entertainment is a statue of George M Cohen that looks towards Times Square on 5th Avenue. George appears to be pointing towards Roy Rogers Steak Bar.

It is the early Twenties and the crowds are moving from one theatre to another; even in those days, tickets sold well above their face value for the early evening performance. The Adelphi Theatre matinee of the musical *About a Quarter to Nine* had just finished. There was no early evening performance of this show so the stars had a few hours to spare. The main star of this musical is none other than Al Jolson, who is in his dressing room. The usual crowd have congregated, leaving Al without much room to get changed. George Miller pushes two song sheets under Al's nose.

"Al, I would like you to sing these two numbers in your next show."
"Who are the writers?" enquires Al.
"Jacobson and Isaacs."
"I'm in a hurry now, George, I'll listen to them tomorrow. If they are any good, you can make the writers Jacobson, Isaacs and Jolson. I'm off now to grab a bit of the action at the Royal. I'm interested in the show *Penny Arcade*."

Yes, Al Jolson is always interested in making money, always insisting that his name appeared on new scores so that he can claim extra royalties. He arrives at the Royal to be met by Les Sibley, the manager. They watch the early performance of the play which delights Al, prompting him to make a proposition to Sibley.

"I would like to buy the film rights of the play, the money will help the show through its difficult patch."

The two shake hands and *Penny Arcade* is on its way to Hollywood. Al

Jolson has beaten the Hollywood producers to the punch! He insists that the two stars of the stage play are cast in the movie and arranges with the stars to receive a percentage of their salaries. The pay is more money than one of the stars of the show has ever seen in his life and he jumps at the chance. This star is none other than James Cagney! He and his co-star Joan Blondell are about to capture Hollywood. At last it is beginning to happen for Jimmy.

James Cagney was born on 17 July 1899 on the East Side of New York. He thought he had reached the pinnacle when he made it on Broadway in his home town but now – Hollywood! Jimmy had had a hard life on the East Side. His father had taught him to defend himself and he was not afraid to take on those twice his size. He never looked for trouble but was always wary of the quiet ones.

"Never worry about the loud mouths or the braggers, their mouths are their only strengths, they are easy" was his dad's sound advice and it made Cagney tough. He had a loving family upbringing and it was a great loss to the family when his father died due to a drink problem. Jimmy worked very hard in three part-time jobs to help his family. The only breadwinner, his education had to take a back seat. He was a very good baseball player, his only opportunity to relax in between running from one part-time job to another. Because one job was as a bouncer, he frequented a gym where he was told that he was good enough to take up boxing professionally.

Jimmy then met a girl, Willard Vernon, who was struggling to make a career in show business and she encouraged him to develop his flair for dancing. Willard had more faith in him than he had in himself and he started to pick up singing and dancing bit-parts. It was tough going but Jimmy was used to hard work. They both took whatever work was going in vaudeville while they waited for a break. They married, then Jimmy was offered a part at the Royal Theatre which developed into the lead with Joan Blondell. *Penny Arcade* was a good production but had cashflow problems. Jolson's spies informed Al of the theatre's difficulties and Jolson's greed to earn that extra buck from Jimmy Cagney's salary opened the door of Warner Brothers for the little, tough guy.

His first film, *Sinners Holiday* was the Penny Arcade story. Warner Brothers were delighted with him, giving him a second movie before he could catch his breath and then a third. The small print of his contract more or less said he was to be available twenty four hours a day! There were no unions then and Jimmy had many a battle, fighting for his rights with Warner Brothers as he went out of one gangster film and into another before the police sirens had died down. This was before special effects were invented and there were no simulated explosions from bullets as you have today. In the film *Public Enemy*, the director would shout "Duck" as real bullets were fired.

James Cagney's huge talents filled the cinemas, whether he played, gangster, boxer or song and dance man. Off screen, he and Willard led a quiet life, mixing only with the families of Pat O'Brien and Spencer Tracy. They were labelled the Irish Mafia but only in fun.

Jimmy had come a long way from New York's East Side to the glitter of Broadway and Hollywood stardom. When walking down 5th Avenue he was often asked by tourists to stand next to the statue of George M Cohen for a photograph, because of his portrayal of Cohen in *Yankee Doodle Dandy*. Jimmy left us in 1986 aged eighty seven. He is up there with his mother and father. He greets them with the same exuberance; "I'm on top of the world, Ma."

He sold hundreds of millions of records and was among the top ten movie stars for over twenty years. He had the Midas touch even during his teenage college days. He was in every sports team and was certainly a fine athlete, as much at home in the board room as he was on the fairway. But it is his family life which concerns many of his fans. We are led to believe that he was a very strict disciplinarian who could be very cold-hearted and cruel to his children. But he could also charm the birds out of the trees with a whistle. While he was at college he learned to play the drums, developing a nice style and joining the Al Rinkler seven piece band. When five of the band left only Al and Harry, who had protruding ears, remained. The 'in' comic-paper of the day was The Bingsville Bugle, whose main character, who also had protruding ears, was called Bingo. So Harry Lilis Crosby was nicknamed Bing.

When Al and Bing decided to go it alone, as two men and a piano, the drums were put under wraps. Off they went to Los Angeles. Their routine was good and they got a lot of bookings on vaudeville's B circuit. As they got better they moved on to the more sophisticated clubs, started getting good reviews in Variety magazine and toured with the great Paul Whiteman, the top band of the day. By 1927, the duo was getting rave notices and brought in Harry Ferras, a songwriter, becoming a trio called the Rhythm Boys that was under the wing of Paul Whiteman. The movie *The King of Jazz* featured Whiteman and the boys. Crosby was now coming to the fore as a solo artiste and, after the movie, it was Crosby who was accompanied by Al Rinkle and Harry Levis at venues such as the Coconut Grove.

During his odd movie spots, he met a film star called Dixie Lee. Dixie, who was near the top, was advised to keep away from Crosby because he would ruin her career. Crosby was a near-alcoholic, or a very heavy drinker, if there is any difference. He was nicknamed the 'Fallen-down Drunk'. When Dixie's friends and family gave her an ultimatum; "Don't bring that drunk into our houses," she left them to marry Bing, putting her career on the line. No-one expected Bing to get any further than the gutter that he was often thrown into from many bars. He had lost the rave notices that he had had a few years ago and was now another also-ran. Even his marriage to Dixie Lee was announced in the press "Top film star Dixie Lee to marry singer Bing Cronby.

It was 1931 and Crosby's lateness and failure to turn up for shows caused friction with the night club owners. They disciplined Bing and the Rhythm Boys, causing a walk out by the trio. They were blacklisted, causing the trio to split. Bing was now on his way to a solo career. He moved into comedy, singing and acting in Max Stennett's slapstick movies like *Dream House,* singing old hits like *When I Take My Sugar to Tea* and *Sitting in a Bath Full of Soap* and performing circus stunts with lions, singing *I Surrender Dear*. When radio became interested in his voice, a CBS manager thought Crosby to be unreliable but was over-ruled and Crosby was signed for fifteen hundred dollars a week, when the norm was only one hundred dollars. His first big broadcast was a no-show because of drink. It was re-scheduled for three days later and a twenty four hour watch was put on Crosby. As the song says, *Just One More Chance* and it worked.

Bing Crosby was the biggest thing on radio for the next thirty years. He had a request programme for his songs alone, something no other artiste has ever achieved. Besides his CBS radio shows, he was booked at the Paramount Theatre for a record revue of twenty seven weeks. Paramount decided to sign him for a three year contract of five films and Bing returned to Hollywood to make his first full-length movie, *The Big Broadcast of 1932.* At about this time, Bing and Dixie started a family with a boy Gary, named after Gary Cooper. Three other boys followed. Jack Kapp of Decca Records signed Bing up to record for his budget price label and persuaded him to sing different types of songs, ballads, religious, country and western and jazz.

While on tour at New York's Capital Theatre, he met a comedian by the name of Bob Hope and they began to collaborate on the radio circuit.

Bing told Bob that he could get him three hundred sailors to provide an audience for Bob's radio theatre show. What he didn't tell him was that they were all off a Dutch ship! Bob died a death but it was all in good fun.

By now, Bing owned a baseball team, a racing track and, golf academies. With Bob Hope, he started pro-am golf tournaments and, in 1940, they starred together in *Road to Singapore*. The *Road* pictures took them from Singapore to Hong Kong over the next twenty years. The film company had their writers and Bob and Bing had their own. One tried to outwit the other with their writers' help but there was a certain level of ad lib which was completely spontaneous. Bing made forty five films altogether, winning an Oscar in 1944 for his role of Father Chuck O'Malley in *Going My Way*. In 1954, he had an Oscar nomination with *Country Girl*, in which he played a devious alcoholic, a role some critics wrote in which he was playing himself.

Certainly Dixie Lee had got him out of the rut that he was in twenty years earlier. Dixie was his saviour. She lost her family and friends for the man she loved. Sadly, theirs was an unhappy marriage and Dixie became an alcoholic as she watched her children being chastised with a leather belt until it drew blood from each child in turn. While Bing was filming *Little Boy Lost* in England in 1952, Dixie Lee, who had given up her career to take a back seat for Bing, was dying of cancer. Bing arrived back in America only fourteen days before she died.

Bing was a hard man, he loved show business and he dominated it for over thirty years. His last film part was as the alcoholic doctor in the old classic which brought John Wayne to fame, *Stagecoach*. In 1977, Bing went on tour to Europe with the show *Bing and Friends*. He died of a heart attack on a Spanish golf course playing the game that was his first love after show business. Perhaps you could say that this was a fairway to go!

The big, piercing blue eyes look over the screen as her words cut through the smoke of the her cigarette. She brought a new dimension to cigarette smoking (as if the horrendous amount of smoke in cinemas at that time wasn't bad enough, with seven out of ten members of the public hooked on the weed). but there were other dimensions that she brought to acting that other actresses could not dream of reaching. At one time, she was making four films a year, a big star in a Hollywood world dominated by men. She complained about the scripts, with justification, as in the Thirties a lot of emphasis was put on quantity. She was a great actress, excelling herself when given parts in classic films such as *Now Voyager, Jezebel* and *Dark Victory*.

She was brought to Hollywood by her mother after her parents had divorced. Her mother worked long hours to meet the expense of keeping Bette at Drama School. In 1930, when the time was right, the Davies' hit Hollywood. What caught the attention of the movie moguls was her ability to act, her dominance and her line learning capability. She knew her lines backwards and those of everyone else! She made over eighty films in the space of six decades. Most of her scenes were on a one-to-one basis and when this was the case, the male did not have much to say! It was so easy for the director, it was a take in one.

The picture *Of Human Bondage* was her big break but she had to go to another studio, away from Warner Brothers who did not get on with her. Jack Warner let her do the picture in the hope that it might be her ruin. In the event, nothing was further from the truth, it made her a star. *Of Human Bondage* was turned down by a dozen stars because they thought that it would have taken away their glamourous images. Bette was on her way, losing ground slightly when Vivian Leigh was successful in getting to play Scarlet O'Hara in *Gone with the Wind*. She climbed back to the top with an Academy Award winner, *Jezabel* and gained her second Oscar. In my opinion, had the story-lines of her movies been more worthy of her acting ability, she would have ended up with more Oscars than anyone else.

Her last picture was *The Wales of August* in 1987. She carried on acting for as long as she could. Right up to the end of her life, at the age of eighty one, she was as sharp as a needle.

When I see aggravating smoke in a cinema today , I am reminded of that generated by Bette. A gimmick, you may say, in those early movies but she was an actress who did not need gimmicks. She reached the pinnacle of her profession.

Familiar screams from the bedroom echo across the large garden and penetrate the night air. They are easily recognisable to the other households in the area. Pedestrians on the main thoroughfare come to a halt, their evening strolls disturbed by the high-pitched screeches.

"Oh no, not again" cries a neighbour. "The poor girl, why doesn't she leave him?"

Another blow sends the attractive blonde sprawling bodily across the dressing table, scattering the expensive perfumes and other articles across the room. Doris dressed only in underwear, is heavily blood-stained from her battered face. She tries to reach the door handle in an attempt to escape from the clutches of her husband, Al Jordan, a trombone player with the Tommy Dorsey Band.

He had met Doris while on tour. She was an excellent singer who used her talents freelancing with the best orchestras of the day. Al Jordan was a schizophrenic, loving one minute and abusive the next. It was during one of his loving spells that he and Doris fell for one another, meeting between sessions and band calls but, once they were married, he had fits of jealousy about the other members of the band, getting paranoid about them having more playtime than he did in certain solo arrangements. This paranoia started to show during performances in his irritation over minor details. This, of course, had an effect on his own performance and he was asked to do less. Little did he know that all this worry and jealousy was causing acute tension which was affecting his memory. He could not remember conversations which had taken place only a week earlier. He would leave sessions in such a state of worry, with a knot in his stomach so intense that by the time he got home he was in a rage. Then Doris became his punch bag.

Doris' hands slip from the door handle as a brogue shoe crashes into her ribs. The kick is so violent that blood flows from her mouth. She lapses into unconsciousness. That was the last time Al Jordan was to lay a finger on Doris.

The sunlight breaks through the blinds of the City Hospital. The ward is filled with enough flowers to fill a high street florist. The brightness of the sun forces Doris to shield her eyes with her bandaged hands, a good sign, for when she had been admitted with both eyes closed it was thought that her sight had been affected. Along with her relatives, stars from stage and screen flock to be by the side of Doris Day, born Doris Von Kappelhoff in Cincinnati, Ohio, in 1924.

This is the first day she has been allowed this many visitors and now she is tired after all the excitement. Doris settles down for the night and remembers the first time that she was admitted to hospital. It was two years after her parents had separated, when she was thirteen years-old. From a very early age, she had shown great skill as a dancer and by the time she reached her teens she was so good, her mother decided to take her to Hollywood. She would have to leave all her friends and it was they who decided to give her a going-away party. Returning home from the party, the car in which she and three of her friends were travelling, hit a train. The front passengers went through the windscreen and Doris's leg was shattered by the front seat, ending her dancing career. After months of being encased in plaster from hip to toe, she tried to dance and all the good work was undone when her leg shattered once more. She was in plaster for another year and it was during this time, when she could no longer dance that, out of boredom, she began singing.

So the beautiful, bubbly blonde, Doris Day, started to captivate the airwaves and moved on to the big bands. Hollywood film studios were soon in the chase and she was soon starring in her first movie, *Romance on the High Seas*, for Warner Brothers. Though we remember her for her many bubbly, musical-comedy classics like *It's Magic, Calamity Jane* and *On Moonlight Bay*, we must not forget her qualities as an actress, including her partnership with James Cagney in *Love Me or Leave Me* and James Stewart in Hitchcock's *The Man Who Knew Too Much*. She turned out recording hits like confetti, most of them coming from her films. One of my favourites was her hit *The Deadwood Stage*, which was coupled with *Secret Love*.

The love and romance that was such a feature in her films and records seemed to elude her in real life. One husband had savagely abused her and another, who was also her business manager and financial adviser, died while still young. Doris had made millions from her records and films and her fortune had been invested into trust funds. She was always assured that they were doing well but her husband's death proved that the trust funds were not sound, in fact they were empty. Investments in hotels and companies were worthless and the bottom line was that Doris owed half a million dollars! Her house was put up for sale to cover unpaid taxes. With good lawyers at her side, she battled on for five years, recovering bits and pieces from her investment fund. The judges vindicated her and awarded her nearly twenty three million dollars, the sun shining through once more.

Doris is now getting her just reward after her ill-fated life. She is happy with her animals in Multi Aora Sanctuary. Looking back on her life, she just says "Que sera, sera".

The young American patrolman was filling in his log book just off Highway 99, outside Los Angeles when his concentration was disrupted by a vehicle that sped past. He immediately followed, gaining on the Porsche, although it took several miles to catch up with it. The patrolman indicated to the driver to pull over. The youth laughed as he accepted the ticket that was forced into his hand.

"I shall be watching out for you." said the patrolman as the driver sniggered as he passed the ticket to his passenger. The Porsche Spyder shot out of sight before the patrolman could get back on his bike and continued north, reaching the car's limit of 130 mph, screeching round bends, the driver's knuckles white on the wheel. Rold Wutherick, the passenger, told him to take it easy.

The driver slowed down. He thought about the last two hectic years in which he had completed the three films that had made him a Hollywood icon. Women adore his sultry looks, his sideburns, the cigarette which trembled from his bottom lip. He was a new breed of actor, his style being imitated by the youths of the day. The mileometer on the Porsche was again creeping up to 90 mph and Rold reminded him;

"It is not important to get there an hour earlier but it is important to get there at all!"

James Dean eases off the accelerator and the car slows to 50 mph and his thoughts wander to his childhood. He was nine years of age when he lost his mother through cancer. It was left to the guidance of the local church and relatives to see James through his schooling and on to college. It was while James was at college, at the age of sixteen, that he had a homosexual relationship with a minister, an affair which lasted several years. There was no guidance from his father who had always worked a good distance from home.

From his college days, James had performed in many amateur plays. He often angered his producers and directors with his many pranks, moods and sulky tantrums. His dream was to become a Hollywood star.

He had now reached the pinnacle of his dreams. It wasn't like this when he first moved to Los Angeles. He got bit parts in commercial and theatre work and was often broke, relying on friends to put him up and to lend him money. One of these friends was an advertising executive, Roger Bracket, fifteen years his senior, who gave him a room in his house. They became passionate lovers. Roger was also a friend of the agent, Henry Wilson, another homosexual, whose gay clients included Rock Hudson, a film star James did not like. They had appeared together in *Giant*, one of his blockbusters. The film had just been completed as he sped north in his new Porsche.

He had always been interested in high-speed driving. He boasted "I had a big bike before Brando" (a major rival). Both the bike and black leathers were part of their trademarks but now Dean's high-speed kicks were experienced on four wheels. He was quite happy being surrounded by women and he had several affairs with the opposite sex during his affair with Roger Bracket.

James Dean earned his chance for a film test which gave him his first picture *East of Eden*. While on set, he met Piers Angeli, who was appearing in another picture *The Silver Chalice* along with newcomer Paul Newman. James and Piers took every opportunity to be with one another, even in between scenes of both pictures. Close friends say Piers Angeli was Dean's only love.

Dean was very difficult to work with and angered his co-stars and producers by walking off the set and being late for work – and this was his first film! He was called Mr Prima Donna. It makes one wonder what hold he had on the film moguls to be able to behave like that. He would throw tantrums, leave his friends sitting in a restaurant while he went on to eat at another on his own. Hedda Hopper, the famous columnist, witnessed his behaviour in a restaurant frequented by the stars. He ordered a meal, walked over to the framed pictures of the stars, spat at the photographs and laughed. He then ate his meal in a piggish manner, putting his plate under his chin.

Pier Angeli refused to elope with Dean and later announced her engagement to Vic Damone. Dean was devastated. Thoughts of Pier and Damone gripped his chest like a vice.

Before long, he was in the arms of another male, his co-star Sal Mineo, but he demonstrated his protest about Angeli and Damone's wedding by revving his motor bike outside the church. Barbara Hutton, the Woolworth's heiress, comforted Dean for the next few months. Defenceless against his charms, she said "it seemed the right thing to do." Natalie Wood, another of his co-stars in *Rebel Without a Cause* then stepped in to give him more comfort. Elizabeth Taylor, the star in *Giant*, liked to mother him but there was no affair. The females came and went, one starlet after another. The men also took their turn in the queue and this time one was going with him on vacation.

The Porsche ate up the miles as they neared their destination. What thoughts crossed James' mind as his foot pushed harder on the pedal causing the Porsche to scream on full throttle at one hundred and ten miles per hour? As he approached the intersection of highways 466 and 41, just outside Bakersfield on Friday night, 30 September 1955, James Dean, aged twenty four, hit another car which was about to cross the intersection. He tried to brake but it was too late. His passenger was thrown clear, receiving only broken bones and the other driver suffered only bruising. But James Dean died, almost decapitated. So passed a *Giant*, in fact, a *Rebel Without a Cause*.

A **stooped, grey-haired figure** presses the doorbell of the Paris flat. A moment passes and it is pressed again. He stands waiting in the corridor, still easily recognisable though well into his seventies. James Stewart waits until eventually the door, which is secured by a brass chain, opens a little. Peering out of the shadows was another famous face, half covered by a black chiffon scarf. She refuses to let Mr Stewart enter. They had known each other for half a century and he had expected a welcome and a lingering kiss, but not now. She was in pain because of the many fractures the brittle bones beneath her wrinkled skin had suffered. She couldn't bear a man who had once viewed her fabulous body with pleasure to see her now. She closes the door and Mr Stewart walks away, bemused. She returns to the comfort of her chair, distressed from the constant pain. She runs her fingers through her limp and thinning hair while she waits for her maid to return from the shops with another batch of drugs. An open photograph album stares depressingly at her from the coffee table and she sheds a tear as she looks at her once fabulous figure and her beautiful looks.

Marie Magdalene Dietrich was born at the turn of the century, the exact date not known, in Schoneberg, Germany. Her father was a military man who brought up his daughter with a good education, her favourite subjects being French and literature. She studied at the Weimar Conservatory. She was also an accomplished violinist but an injury to a finger ended the possibility of her becoming a concert star. Being a good reader, she auditioned for plays and even silent films. Wherever she made an entrance, everyone stopped what they were doing to admire her beauty. She also had remarkable, eye-catching dress sense. In her first film, she affected a monocle belonging to her father, sowing the seed of a legend. The monocle trademark was at that time used by the gays and lesbians of the underworld. She then sported trousers. Within a short time, Marlene and her trademarks were known throughout the world with all the magazines emphasising her remarkable beauty. She married Rudi Sieber, a production assistant and they had a little girl and were proud to parade their lovely baby in the parks. But soon the glamour of the theatre and screen brought the marriage to an end.

Marlene had become an enigma in Germany. It was the Roaring Twenties and America was rolling out the red carpet for this continental beauty. Rumours about her sexuality gained momentum throughout her career. She was linked to many a female star including Claudette Colbert and Lili Damita (who was to become Mrs Errol Flynn). Some biographers claim she was anti-gay, whilst her own daughter's book, published after Marlene's death, details how she took women to bed. Once, while travelling to America in the Thirties, she became friendly with a woman passenger. The passenger was quite proud to be in the company of such a famous star until Marlene produced a book on lesbian love when they went to Marlene's cabin for a drink. The passenger made a quick exit.

In America, the studio sets fell silent when she made her entrance, the men stood open-mouthed at her electrifying beauty. In her picture *Blue Angel* Marlene mesmerised all in a top hat, silk stockings and black suspenders, crooning the melody which became her hallmark, *Falling in Love Again.* Her leading man was upstaged by her and, in the scene in which he is supposed to strangle her, he was so upset that he nearly killed her. The stage-hands had to drag him off and she had marks on her neck for weeks. This tension remained throughout filming. The film was a great success, Miss Dietrich had arrived. The publicity put Marlene right on top of the popularity polls, bringing her a salary of $350,000. Hitler asked her to return to Berlin, to join him in an open-topped parade and also to join him in bed! Yes, everyone fancied Marlene Dietrich and she loved every minute of her popularity. She loved the gossip as one affair followed another. She went from Gary Cooper to Maurice Chevalier. Of Chevalier she said "I adored him, he was the finest man I've ever loved." John Wayne was not to be outdone. She invited him into her dressing room, he locked the door behind him. "What's the time?" she asked, then answered her own question by raising her skirt to reveal a garter watch, saying "Yes, we have time!" She didn't want to be late for dinner with Douglas Fairbanks Junior and with Frank Sinatra, who was also a suitor. During World War II, she bedded two American generals, Patton and Gavin. The French heart-throb, Jean Gabin, was next in line to experience the charms of the German bombshell.

Age was becoming an issue and her lovers were becoming much younger. Michael Wilding, eleven years her junior, walked out on her to marry Elizabeth Taylor who was thirty years her junior. She was devastated. She also shared Mike Todd with Elizabeth before Taylor married him. She was obsessed with Yul Brynner during a six-year affair but he then went back to his wife. Burt Bacharach was next, she was twenty seven years older than him. Their relationship flourished for some time but Angie Dickinson caught Burt's fancy, leaving Marlene livid. She quoted "To marry her, he might as well marry Julie Andrews!" She was by now concerned about her age, moving to Switzerland for rejuvenating therapy. For many, reaching seventy would be the time to retire, but not Marlene. She was always on the lookout for a loving relationship, no matter which sex. While on stage she wore a rubber body-suit and still looked a million dollars. Even at this age the suitors were knocking on her dressing room door.

But now she is behind the door of her Paris flat trying to dull the pain. A drop of whisky in her tea may help. Her maid serves her the drink. This could have been the time to tell the maid "See what the boys in the back room will have," but alas, there are no boys, the room is empty. The family album falls to the floor, scattering the snaps. The loves of her life now lie at her feet once more. She is dead at the age of ninety one.

He was labelled the perfect English gentleman, he may have become greater than the masculine Leslie Howard, more refined than Olivier. Yes, he could have been the greatest English actor to cross the Atlantic to America. In his twenty five years as a film actor he made classic movies which are shown time and time again on the small screen. When one of his movies is mentioned it is remembered as a classic. The reason that this actor made so many classic films is that he only made nineteen during his twenty five year career because of bad health. Many times he had to turn down major roles because of his chronic asthma and if it wasn't his asthma, it was his stammer or nervous breathlessness.

Robert Donat, the son of a Pole, was born in Manchester in 1905. By the time the First World War was over, illness had limited his acting but he was determined to establish himself and never gave up trying in his aim for the top. He had elocution lessons to control his stammer and by 1930 they paid off. He had joined the Frank Benson London Company of Actors and was making a name for himself, breaking into British films with Alexander Korda in 1932. He was an immediate success and the offers rolled in. But as the parts grew bigger the burden became greater. Those hard days toiling on the film set, sometimes taking two days for just one scene, brought on asthma attacks. Tears would fill his eyes as he tried to bring out his lines, his lungs gasping for more air. Time and time again, filming was postponed as oxygen cylinders were brought to his rescue. A less determined man would have given up because of the heartbreaking and embarrassing situations. But no, he was a good actor and everyone on the set knew he was destined to be one of the greatest.

Robert Donat always hoped that someday a cure would be found for his chronic ailment but his handicap did not deter the producers and directors. During the 1930s, Donat kept busy reading script after script, only to turn most of them down as he knew he was just not up to it. He would wait, hoping that on the next day he might feel a bit better. He would be filled with despair when a script he had read months before was made into a film and became a success. He would stammer out his words of concern, desperately trying to hide the tears in his eyes. To try to detail the number of films that Donat had had to pass on to other up-and-coming stars would be impossible. Because of his problems, many a star got their big break. We must be grateful that his health stayed stable enough for him to make such classic movies as *The Count of Monte Cristo, The Thirty Nine Steps, The Young Mr Pitt, The Citadel,* and his Oscar-winning performances in the weepy *Goodbye Mr Chips* and *The Magic Box*. It was when playing the part of the camera inventor, Friese Green, in *The Magic Box*, that he played a scene where he ran into the street with his first developed photograph in order to get someone to witness it. The first person that he found was a policeman, who was being played by Laurence Olivier!

I have named only a few of the nineteen films that Donat made during those illness-plagued years. Had his life not been marred by ill health, you can imagine what heights Robert Donat could have reached. In 1958 Robert was to star with Ingrid Bergman in *The Inn of the Sixth Happiness* as a Christian convert in a Chinese monastery. This was to be his last film. He was too ill to contemplate taking on the part but he was determined to do it as he knew he was dying. Indeed everyone on the set knew he was dying, as did most of the film world. Each scene was treated with respect in honour of this great actor. Some of the actors broke down as they tried to remember their lines, their voices breaking with emotion as actresses wept behind the scenes. Robert was nursed through his lines but his brilliance shone through and it became very emotional for everyone as the picture neared completion.

On the last day of shooting, Robert Donat walked off the set, knowing that it was goodbye. He was about to climb his own thirty nine steps.

The middle-aged man was calling for his son as he lay dying "Please come back, I miss you." His wife tries to comfort him, giving him more medication to ease the pain. He relaxes into a semi-sleep, thinking about the boy his beloved wife gave birth to in Cedar Rapids, Iowa, in 1937. He was a beautiful baby with big blue eyes, eyes that when they looked at you made you want to hold and cuddle him. He started to grow up just as lovely, with a mop of curly hair, his eyes just as inviting. The neighbours always stopped and talked to little Bobby. "He will break many a heart when he grows up" was the usual cry from the boy's admirers.

The family decided to move from Iowa to California when Bobby was six. By now his golden locks were a bit on the long side. The barber took to little Bobby immediately.

"This kid's cute, just look at those eyes. He should be in pictures. A lot of my customers work over in MGM, they tell me they are always auditioning kids for future movies."

Mum and Dad took the barber's advice and went to the studios. The barber certainly knew what he was talking about. Young Bobby was hired on the spot to star with Margaret O'Brien, the child sensation of the day in the film *Lost Angel*. Margaret O'Brien was one of the child stars who never graduated to adult roles. Bobby was a great success, when it came to memorising his lines he was a natural. His acting was even better. He was put alongside great stars such as Ann Baxter, Veronica Lake, Lillian Gish, Myrna Loy, Allan Ladd and Don Amechie. Myrna Loy said of Bobby, "This kid will keep us on our toes, if not, he will take the limelight." Because of his age he was able to move from studio to studio, every producer wanted him and more stars were of Myrna Loy's opinion. Bobby was becoming big box office. He showed off his incredible acting ability with George Sanders, Corneal Wilde, Charles Boyer and Robert Preston.

In 1946 he signed a contract with Walt Disney to star in *Song of the South*, a story about little Johnny who is always running away from home but is encouraged to stay by the stories told by Uncle Remus. "You can't always be running away, Johnny, there is no place like home." The stories of love and affection made *Song of the South* a real blockbuster. It was a great success when it was reissued in 1956 and again in 1972. I think this should be amongst the films that are released on video by Disney year after year: a Disney classic lying in the archives. He made five more pictures for Disney, making millions of dollars for the animation corporation.

In 1950, Bobby came to England to give a great performance as Jim Hawkins in *Treasure Island*. It was a smash hit, even bigger than Jackie Cooper's version of 1934. His voice was used for an animated version of *Peter Pan*. Bobby Driscoll was certainly a great favourite but now the real Peter Pan of Hollywood was growing up. He became surly and grumpy and his once adorable looks were overtaken by acne which became a problem. His short marriage to Marilyn Bush ended in separation. By 1956, at the age of nineteen, he was on a downhill slide with drugs becoming a big part of his life. He was arrested on several occasions, dressed in torn jeans, did not bother to wash and his teeth became loose. Though he had a high IQ, his brain was affected. Bobby had travelled a long way since he triumphed in the movie *The Window*. It is a poor image of Bobby Driscoll who is booked for assault with a deadly weapon, the handcuffs hiding some of the scars that are embedded in his wrist from the injection needles. Money had been his downfall – he had the money to pay for the kicks.

Bobby Driscoll dropped out of sight after his release from prison. He drifted from town to town, his parents not knowing where he was. They would have cried if they had seen him amongst the bums and tramps of New York, as he wandered into derelict buildings for a night's sleep.

A night's sleep is what his father now needs as he thinks of his childhood-star son and wonders about his whereabouts. Will he see him before he dies? Mrs Driscoll contacts the FBI in the search for Bobby but no trace of him comes to light. Was he in a mental hospital with brain damage not knowing who he was? The FBI contacted the Disney Corporation for Bobby's fingerprints. Eighteen months earlier, on March 30th., 1968, two children playing in a deserted tenement in New York came across the corpse of a young man that was surrounded by religious effects. Fingerprints were taken from the heavily injected arms. The body was not identified and therefore buried in a pauper's grave without a name. It was later found to be the body of Bobby Driscoll.

Disney re-released *Song of the South*, making more money than ever before. Uncle Remus's story in the film, as told to the young Bobby Driscoll, was included. Had Bobby taken heed of those tales he would have seen his father alive again. His father hears the news of Bobby's death and thinks of what might have been. If only ... if only ... his thoughts are of Bobby's first picture, *Lost Angel*. "How fitting" he murmers, "I shall find him soon!"

The young actor was waiting patiently on his horse for the director to give the command "Action." Two heavy stunt men crept up behind the horse and crudely, with a large object, made the horse rear-up then bolt across the set at speed, with the actor hanging on in fear of being seriously injured. Our actor, himself a practical joker, did not think much of this joke. He returned to the set to confront the two very large men who had been responsible. They were later rushed to hospital, neither being able to work for at least two months. Yes, the handsome, flamboyant Errol Flynn had made his mark on Hollywood, as well as on the stunt men.

Errol Flynn was born in Hobart, Tasmania, off the coast of Australia in 1909. His mother was a descendant of one of the mutineering sailors from the Bounty. The sword he played with as a child on his grandfather's yacht once belonged to Fletcher Christian. He was highly sexed and at a very early age was caught by his mother playing mummies and daddies. As a teenager he left home for New Guinea, wanting adventure. The adventure turned out to be sleeping with native women and working on plantations. A film producer spotted him and gave him a part in a film, ironically about mutineers. The acting bug had got to Erroll and he sailed for England, landing a part in *Murder in Monte Carlo*. The director, Irving Asher, saw that Flynn had a future and sent him to Hollywood to see Jack Warner. His first part in Hollywood was as a corpse in *The Curious Bride*, a funny title for Flynn who never really wanted a bride, only a woman. His second wife, Nora Eddington, once said Errol never had an affair because he only stayed with them for three days!

His first marriage to Lily Domita broke up when he reached stardom. He moved into a bachelor pad by the sea with David Niven. The traffic in female companionship was very heavy. As I said before, Erroll was a practical joker. Once he got a studio technician to make him a false piece of anatomy which he hid under a towel he was wearing. He invited a director and actor Alan Hale into his caravan dressing-room to talk about a possible change in the next scene, which involved him just wearing a towel. He suggested dropping the towel in the scene and proceeded to rehearse in the caravan. Alan Hale took one look and said "I'll have a pound and a half." Perhaps it was because of this story we hear of the possibly exaggerated physique of Mr Flynn which obviously suited his lifestyle as the women swarmed to him like a plague of locusts.

From his first big break as the lead in *Captain Blood*, he became big box office and followed up with the big hits *The Charge of the Light Brigade, Robin Hood* and *They Died with their Boots On*. I remember the great fencing duel he had with Basil Rathbone in *Robin Hood*. It was so lifelike, I think he really wanted to kill Rathbone. He probably did as Flynn was only on a fraction of the established star's salary. After this it was a different story. Flynn could command the highest salaries Hollywood had ever paid and his lifestyle was flamboyant and extravagant. He bought a yacht, Saga, and young starlets visited it on a daily basis. At his mansions he had scores of parties. Stars who were invited to spend weekends would witness the double mirrors, viewing couples watching pornographic movies. One critic claims Flynn lived the life of at least six men and drinks and drugs started to make him look and feel old by the time he was fifty. Mickey Rooney said of Flynn "Erroll woke up one morning and found he was no longer Robin Hood." Flynn died of a heart attack when he was fifty three. If he did live the life of six men, what a way to live for three hundred years! Years after Flynn's death, David Niven passed a ship-repair yard and noticed a very familiar broken-down yacht, Saga, lying in a corner, beyond repair. Saga – a fitting name, meaning peace.

Erroll Flynn's name is cemented with a brass star in the star-studded pavement in Hollywood. As the sun comes up, the building opposite throws a shadow across the pavement. The building, a theatre which shows blue movies, leaves the once brightly, neon-lit name of Eroll Flynn in the dark.

The hint of strength behind the smile and the occasional wink brought out the best of his handsome face. He was like Jack Dempsey in a tuxedo and his female fans loved his every movement. His moustache would twitch before his mouth opened to produce a smile which would fill the full width of the screen. Men all over the world tried to imitate him in style and appearance. The pencil-slim moustache had never been so popular.

In one of his Oscar-winning performances in *It Happened One Night* in 1934, he takes his shirt off in a bedroom scene. Millions of cinema-goers witnessed that he wore no vest! Companies around the world who made this garment either went bankrupt or had to adapt to manufacturing a suitable replacement product. He would be seen with a string of film lovelies. If you hadn't been seen with William Clark Gable, you were a nobody. Many female stars were in love with him and would openly say so. Joan Crawford said that the impact of being near him brought on twinges of sexual urges beyond belief. Their affair helped each of them in their careers. Other stars who could not get into his bed made comments like "They were like lower-class animals performing in a first-class hotel" and "Her eyes were filled with lust for him." Their affair was open and even by today's standards would have been given a treble-X certificate.

Clark was born in 1901 and had a variety of jobs in and around Hollywood before he became a movie extra. When he did get a screen test it was a failure but he persevered and got into a Western in 1931, *The Painted Desert*, thus gaining a contract with MGM that was to last for the next twenty three years. By 1932, he was a star. When he was photographed for the press there was a girl on each arm and his trademark grin could have been saying "Right girls, who's next?" In between his flings there were two marriages, although I don't suppose these put a stop to his obliging nature!

He was making four movies a year for Metro but he did not think much of the story lines and started to ask for better material. While this was happening, he killed a woman through drunk-driving. A Metro executive took the blame and went to jail so that Gable could be loaned-out to Columbia to make the Oscar-winning film *It Happened One Night*. A very apt title, don't you agree? That was something he had to live with. 1934 was his best year with four good pictures, one being *Manhattan Melodrama*. This was the last picture that Dillinger watched before being gunned down by the police outside the cinema. It was also the breakthrough for a young Mickey Rooney. All this fame in the year which should have seen him in jail.

Other great movies which were to follow during the Thirties were *Call of the Wild*, the Jack London classic, *Mutiny on the Bounty*, *San Francisco* and *Gone with the Wind*. You will be interested to know that Gable was one of the few not to receive an Oscar for this epic. He upset a lot of people in its making and would not talk with a Southern accent. He also got the first director fired. In the making of the film, he uttered the now famous line "Frankly, my dear, I don't give a damn" and that attitude was typical of Gable.

He met Carol Lombard in 1939 and she became his third wife. He really loved her and she seemed to change his arrogant attitude. Yes, he was deeply in love for the first time and was a broken man when she was killed in an air crash in 1942. This was the start of his decline and he went into shock and out of the public eye for about three years. His popularity sank. The man of the moment in Hollywood was now Humphrey Bogart. Gable stayed at home nursing a broken heart. In 1945 he came out of hiding and steadily eased himself back into the limelight. He appeared sadder, the merriment gone from his smile. In 1947, he was back at the top again, making *Stolen Hours*. When it was finished and in the cutting room to be edited, he was in Mexico working on his next film. The director in charge of editing *Stolen Hours* noticed an extra in the court room scene, a blonde who looked remarkably like Carol Lombard.

Clark Gable was summoned back to Hollywood to observe the findings. He ran out of the room when he saw the clip crying "It's my

Carol, she's come back." And it was Carol Lombard, although the actress had been dead for five years! An investigation was made and it was discovered that previously unused backdrops of some old movies, in which Carol Lombard had been an extra, had been used for some of the court scenes of *Stolen Hours*. The scenes were never re-made and Gable paid the studio $200,000 to compensate them for their lost revenue. *Stolen Hours* was buried away in the celluloid graveyard.

Gable made *The Misfits* in 1960 with Marilyn Monroe but he didn't live long enough to see its release. He died of a heart attack just before the birth of his only son to his fifth wife. Finally, time had stolen hours on him!

The expectant mother moves slowly around the house, careful not to disturb her two daughters who are tucked up in bed, they had been singing together earlier in the evening as part of the family act, the mother being a professional with her husband. While she was carrying their third child she had to leave the entertaining to her other half who was downtown at one of the many clubs doing his solo spot. Mrs Gumm sits waiting for him to return. She looks in again at the two Gumm sisters who are sound asleep. She then rests her back which is aching due to the eight and a half month old child she is carrying. She looks at the clock, her husband is late, he should be home by now.

The show finished long ago but Frank Gumm has taken his needs elsewhere. He never goes home right after the show but wanders into the gay bars to see who is available that night. Yes, Frank was a bisexual who still found time to father the three Gumm sisters. Ethel, his wife, knew of his appetite for male sex. Her mind wanders back to the years of struggling to bring up the children in between the hectic nights of variety as they toured the clubs and theatres. Ethel played the piano as Frank sang. Of Irish descent, he had a good voice with deep tones.

Ethel waited and waited, feeling very lonely knowing that her husband was with a man. She tried to comfort herself and the little one inside her, hoping that her baby would never be as lonely in the future as she was then. But how wrong she was to be. The little baby soon to be brought into this world would be singing *Jingle Bells*, her first song on stage, within eighteen months. After that performance, she watched from the wings in her buggy as the Gumm family toured the provinces of Grand Rapids. The Four Gumms, as they were known, appeared on different posters, often with their name misspelt. Frances Ethel Gumm was three years of age when she joined her sisters on stage. One of the misspellings was Glumm – a critic spotted this and in his comments said the girls were far from glum, in fact, they were all as pretty as garlands. From then on they were known as the Garland Sisters, with the young Frances being nicknamed Judy.

We move to 1926. Ethel and Frank Gumm had been pillars of the community until gossip about Frank spread about the town and the family decided to move to Los Angeles. This broke Judy's heart as she loved the town where she had been born. Frank found a job as a projectionist and the sisters kept on singing and appeared at small halls whenever they could. Judy's voice was developing into something special and she stood out from her sisters. Ethel plugged away at the radio stations, knowing that she would soon make her daughters famous. The work was now demanding that the sisters stay in the big city, leaving Frank to his projectionist work which was hours of travel away. This soon parted the family and the marriage as Frank was free to exploit his homosexuality to the full. The newspapers were giving rave reviews to the sisters, especially to the little one, whose style, charisma and outstanding voice opened the door for a solo career. Her sisters were courting and marriage would eventually put an end the trio. Louis B Mayer at MGM had been taking note of Judy's rise to fame and gave her a year's contract. She was an immediate hit with film-goers along with all the other MGM youngsters – Mickey Rooney, Freddie Bartholomew, Peggy Ryan, Deanna Durban and Jackie Cooper. But just before that contract with MGM, Frank died, all alone, in Lancaster, near Los Angeles. He was never to know of his daughter's achievements. Judy did not know that he had been forced to leave the theatre because of mismanagement, leaving debts of thousands of dollars along with whispers and stories of his indiscretions with schoolboys. His death also helped to drive a wedge between Judy and her mother. From then on there was a great war of bitterness which eventually took this star-studded talent away from her millions of fans.

I am not going to mention all the great movies and records that she made – her fans saw those films and bought her records – they know that side of Judy's success and will always remember it. Her achievements and highlights are there for all to see on the back of any LP or CD. Her first movie *Every Sunday Afternoon* with Deanna Durban, was made in 1936 and the rest is history.

Judy, the young individualist, was under pressure to conform to the likes of the leggy beauties of the day who traditionally made it big in Hollywood. She was no glamour girl, her body was out of proportion, her legs being too long for her body. She was also under five-feet tall and was putting on weight. Her own words were "I'm like a little fat pig in pigtails." By the age of seventeen, she had swallowed enough tablets (prescribed by a doctor) to make her a junkie for life. She had been a child star but when she matured, her films struggled. She looked for consolation as she was always lonely. She married David Rose, the orchestra leader of *The Stripper* fame, who was twelve years her senior but after a year Rose asked for a divorce. Vincente Minelli was next and that marriage produced a daughter, Lisa.

MGM decided to part company with Judy, she was difficult to work with, late on the set and always arguing. Judy must have made the youngest comeback of all time when she was only twenty nine years of age. Starring at the London Palladium, she took it by storm and continued a non-stop tour with great success. But then the pills took their toll and she had to rest. The success of her tour opened the door for more movies but though her performances were good, the movies themselves failed to get recognition. The marriage to Minelli was long past when she met Sid Luft. This marriage produced another good singer, Lorna Luft. They parted and reconciled three times before their final parting. Television series and more world tours followed, with extensive rests in between as Judy's health was in a bad state. She contracted hepatitis, a painful kidney infection and had a suspected heart attack. The doctors warned her to ease her intake of pills but her quest for sleep led to the popping of more pills. Her friends were becoming weary of her panic attacks. In 1946, while touring Australia she tripped onto the stage and left in tears after only a handful of songs. A few days later, in Hong Kong, she went into a coma. Mark Herron found her and drove her through a tropical typhoon to the hospital, thus saving her life. They married but it only lasted five months.

She made one final grab at happiness in the last few months of her life when she met Mickey Deans, a disco manager. He seemed to understand her and dedicated himself to her, limiting her to forty pills a day! He took her to her favourite city, London. They enjoyed that June day in 1969, then watched TV and sang at the piano. Mickey had a sore throat and the medicine he was taking made him sleep heavily. He woke to the ringing of the phone. The bed was empty and the bathroom door was locked. He broke the door down to find Judy sitting on the toilet, having taken too many barbiturates. She was dead. Mickey Rooney said "When she sang it was always poetry." Judy was only forty nine years of age. Twenty thousand people filed past her coffin in Madison Square Garden. Judy had reached the end of that yellow brick road, somewhere over the rainbow.

When Marilyn Monroe was a little girl growing up in a foster home, Jean Harlow was the reigning queen of Hollywood. She was the blonde bombshell of the early Thirties, a title Marilyn would inherit twenty years later. Jean Harlow had a lingering smile, blue eyes and was the original the gorgeous-blonde stereotype. When her first major film *Hell's Angels* opened in 1930, Harlow was an overnight success. The famous line from the film "Do you mind if I slip into something more comfortable?" became as well-known as Mae West's "Come up and see me some time." Her career as a star and sex symbol was assured. In 1931, she appeared in five different films. She was to the male movie-goer what Rudolph Valentino was to the female movie fans years before.

Jean was a glamorous blonde who dictated her own salary as she sent her male fans wild. She appeared in all the best magazines and advertising hoardings featuring her in every pose imaginable, enticed the public to buy anything from cigarettes to mattresses. She was the only film star to have a complete set of cigarette cards devoted to her. She was certainly big box-office and her films drew large crowds who queued for hours before the cinemas opened for business. Jean Harlow was at the height of her fame when her death, at only twenty six, shocked a world that had not even registered that she was ill.

Her death was officially attributed to a cerebral haemorrhage but this did not satisfy the world's press who needed stories which were scandalous and, like today, were prepared to listen to anyone who wanted to make them up. In the scandal-laden atmosphere of Hollywood, Jean's death was unofficially attributed to an amazing variety of causes including a botched abortion, heavy drinking, drugs, a damaged kidney that had resulted from a beating by her second husband and photographs taken with a gorilla portraying a beauty and the beast that went wrong with the gorilla raping the beauty.

Harlow's funeral was as much of a tasteless Hollywood production as Valentino's had been a few years earlier. The coffin was smothered in gardenias and lily of the valley and an aeroplane scattering flowers almost drowned out the service. Jeanette Mcdonald sang *Indian Love Call*, Harlow's favourite song. Nelson Eddy sang *Ah! Sweet Mystery of Life* while everyone wept. MGM quickly cashed-in on the publicity by releasing her last film which was a great success, although Harlow would never prove to be as popular in death as some of the other big stars. She set the standards for pin-ups in the years to come. Who knows, without Harlow, would we have seen Mansfield?

Princess Yasmin patiently holds the spoon so that her mother can sip the hot soup, gently dabbing her lips as the soup fails to enter the closed mouth. Tears fill Yasmin's eyes as her mother stares blankly, as if looking beyond the wall of the luxury home. The young princess has been nursing her mother for the last seven years. They are rich and could afford to have the best clinical treatment in the world but Yasmin prefers to take care of her mother herself. It has been a hard struggle for the young girl whose love and devotion has produced such an excellent level of nursing. The time has come when young Yasmin wrestles with the question of whether she should move her mother to a nursing home or persevere; she loves her so much. Yasmin manages to get some food into the old lady, at least enough for the present. In a couple of hours she will start all over again, in between doing all the duties involved in nursing a bedridden patient. She wipes her eyes and tries to make conversation with her mother who still stares blankly ahead. Yasmin puts on a brave smile and switches on the television and video, preparing a selection of video tapes of her mother's old films. She still hopes that maybe, just maybe, one of those classic films might break through that hypnotic stare and bring a real expression to her face – a face which used to have a wide smile and flashing eyes, with a sensuous figure to complete the picture.

That figure made her a forces pin-up in the 1940s when they had nicknamed her the Love Goddess. She had followed in the footsteps of her parents, dancing her way into movies since she was twelve years-old. Yasmin tries to select one of the video tapes, naming the titles in the faint hope that her mother's facial expression might change. Yes, she would try again tomorrow and carry on trying as she had been doing for the last couple of years.

"Right, Mother, which film shall we watch today? What about *Gilda* with Glenn Ford, or maybe *Salome*. Then again, we could watch *The Lady from Shanghai*. I know, we will watch *Separate Tables* with Burt Lancaster." The same ritual was repeated every day, with Yasmine gripping a handkerchief tightly as she tried to stop the sob in her voice, her eyes red and puffy. Her mother will sleep in a moment and Yasmin will retire to another room to have a good cry.

Her mother was born Margarita Carman in 1918, changing her surname to Hayworth and shortening her christian name to Rita. Yes, this once leggy beauty, a cousin of Ginger Rogers, came from a family of dancers. She broke into the Fox Studios in 1935 and made a couple of decent pictures but when Twentieth Century merged with Fox, Rita was reduced to a series of B pictures. Then she met Edward Judson who took her under his wing. As well as marrying her, he brought out her sexiness. He altered her hair style and her dressers introduced a new, classical line. She was back in business as a top star. She was a great dancer and had many singing parts, though her voice was usually dubbed with some up-and-coming songster's. Her marriage to Judson was dissolved and she married Orson Wells in 1943.

It was after this marriage that there was a decline in her work. While still under contract to Twentieth Century Fox she was lent her out to other studios. During her travels with MGM and Universal, she met Prince Ali Khan and eloped with him, breaking her contract which Hollywood frowned upon. She gave birth to a daughter but the glamour of Hollywood soon tempted her back to the lights and action. Rita's fourth marriage to Dick Haymes, one of the top crooners of the day, was just around the corner. She never seemed to find happiness in marriage. She never realised her full potential and took to drink during the decline of her career. I will never forget her dance routine in *Pal Joey*, starring Frank Sinatra; she was a great dancer. The one positive outcome of all her short-lived marriages was Princess Yasmin, from her union with Ali Khan. Yasmin stuck by her in her later years, looking after her with all the love she could give.

The video tape of one of Rita's old films has been played for the last time. Yasmin comforts her mother as she passes away, to suffer no more from the dreaded Alzheimer's Disease. If anyone deserved an Oscar, it was her little girl.

The district of Turtle Bay on New York's East Side was not the most fashionable of areas when the young actress moved into her home in the 1930s. If Elizabeth Taylor is called the Queen, this young starlet went on to become the Queen Mother. She is now in her eighties, still living in the Turtle Bay home which has brought so much happiness and heartbreak. She looks towards the mantlepiece at a photograph of her only love, who died in 1967. He looks across at her, forever smiling. She was with him right to the end and they were together in his last film *Guess Who's Coming to Dinner.* Throughout the filming Spencer Tracy was dying on the set as he forced himself to finish the film which was to give Katherine Hepburn her second Oscar, the first having been in 1933 with *Morning Glory.*

After Spencer Tracy's death, she took the award again the following year with *The Lion in Winter*. This brilliant actress, who notched up sixty years of Hollywood movies, is the only female to win four Oscars, the fourth one coming from *On Golden Pond* with the Fondas in 1981. One of her greatest performances was in *The African Queen* – the person who nominated her thought she should have been presented with the statuette in 1951 when the male award went to her co-star Humphrey Bogart. She was beaten by a great performance from Vivienne Leigh in *A Street Car Named Desire*. Katherine Hepburn made nine films with Spencer Tracy, a great actor in his own right and Katherine's lover for many years. Spencer would never divorce his wife. Katherine said of her relationship with Spencer "It was a unique feeling I had for him. I would have done anything for him."

Today, Turtle Bay is an elite area of New York's East Side. Her neighbour is the great composer, Stephen Sondheim. This is a far cry from those years in the Thirties when she moved in as a young starlet waiting to conquer Broadway. She conquered Hollywood instead. The stars looked up to her, they admired her strong character, her reputation of always getting what she wanted. "If you think you are good enough, let them know you are good enough. Never let them walk all over you, if you do, you will never be appreciated and you will always play second fiddle. I myself will always lead the orchestra, if not conducting it." The grand old lady sits in her living-room, nearing the end of a great innings. Her four Oscars lie hidden in a cupboard out of sight. She only needs the image of her beloved Spencer as he smiles down from the mantlepiece at his *African Queen*.

The morning sunlight breaks through the open curtains and the ageing star shades his eyes from the dazzling rays. This once-handsome man moans as he tries to lift himself from the couch. How long has he been there? What day is it? He does not know. He does not even know what year it is. The empty bottles lie scattered on the floor of his lounge, resembling the scene at a coconut shy. Another drinking binge is over, if only to prepare for the next one. He struggles to the bathroom to witness a nightmare as he peers into the mirror. To his horror, he sees an old man with deep lines embedded in a pain-etched face. He cries, knowing that it was not all that long ago since his handsome face was on the front of all the film magazines. He was a heart-throb but now his face looks like the most used in Hollywood. Alcohol could take most of the credit in making his comparatively young body look like that of a man of ninety.

His mind wanders back to his home town of Pasadena, where he was born in 1918. He emerged from junior college to appear at the local playhouse. Paramount Studio spotted him and put him under contract but it was Columbia that gave him his chance. After making a couple of dozen movies, William Franklyn Beedle finally got his big break but was killed right at the start of the picture. A bullet fracturing his ribs and lungs, he floats face down in a swimming pool, narrating the story of the 1950 smash hit *Sunset Boulevard*. This was the story of has-been film star Norma Desmond, played by Gloria Swanson. Yes, it is the breakthrough that this handsome man needed. Every agent in Hollywood wanted him under their wing. The scripts piled in but he had no time to read them. He had agents to do that for him, his time was precious. Every studio wanted his services, William Holden had arrived with a bang.

He then joined Judy Holliday in making *Born Yesterday*, also in 1950, the film winning an Oscar. He won an Oscar himself as the racketeer sergeant in *Stalag 17*. More good movies were to follow during the 1950s, such as *The Country Girl, Love is a Many Splendoured Thing, The Bridge on the River Kwai* and *The World of Suzy Wong*, to name but a few. Then, in

1969, he appeared in *The Wild Bunch*. The lines were beginning to show and got worse with every picture throughout the Seventies, each line a story on his withered face. The pictures kept coming and he was still able to show off his talents as an actor in *Wild Rover, The Towering Inferno, Network* and *Omen 2*.

How long could he last? His face was looking like a prune. The alcoholism was now taking its toll on his liver as his drinking binges sometimes lasted a week. William Holden had never got over something that happened when he was filming in Europe. While under the influence of drink, he drove a car into a bystander and killed him. He is still looking in the mirror, coming back to reality, his eyes red with tears. What he needs is a drink – maybe just one … or two … or three. He returns to the couch, throwing himself face down, the bottle tightly grasped by the neck. It was *Sunset Boulevard* all over again – but this time he was killing himself! William Holden died in 1981, at sixty three years of age.

It is 1957 and dark clouds settle overhead at the United Artists Studios in Hollywood. A fine drizzle begins to fall. Stage hands rush to protect scenery that is parked against the walls that form the perimeters of the wide avenues of the vast film company. The stars and the extras, dressed in the many variations of attire of the different films being shot, run for cover. The lady in the college party-dress presses the spring on her umbrella, releasing the cover for her protection as she crosses from studio B to her dressing room. She looks upset as she dabs a tissue to her face and suppresses a sob as she runs the rest of the way. Reaching the privacy of the dressing room she flops down, burying her head as she cries herself to sleep. She has just finished the picture *Spring Reunion* and, throughout the making of the film, there have been rows with the director and producer that have extended the time which has been allowed for completion.

A knock on the door of the dressing room and the movie-star Dana Andrews enters the room to console the female star.

"The picture is over now, you needn't ever work for them in the future. There are other studios which will be only too pleased to offer you a contract."

"Yes, I know. It would have been much easier if my husband had directed this movie. He was scheduled to do so and then the producer changed his mind. That is what caused all this trouble. I will never forgive the producer for this."

"Where is your husband?" Dana asks.

"I don't know, he walked out after being fired." The lady is calm once more and Dana leaves her in a better state of mind.

The rain is still coming down as Mr Andrews grips his trilby and runs through the puddles of water into the night. Our star sinks back into the chair and relaxes but her eyes are still red from all the crying. She feels that she has had enough of stardom. Although she is still under contract she feels at the end of her tether. The suitcase is open and all her personal things are packed. A drink settles her nerves. It is no longer raining. The lights of the avenue are reflected in pools of water as she emerges from the doorway, her raincoat matching her beret. The suitcase stands on the step as she shuts the door. The walk towards the studio gate seems to last forever. Though she is leaving she appears to want to wait before she gives her last goodbye to Fred as she passes through security.

"Goodnight, Fred."

"Goodnight, Miss." The gabardine raincoat disappears into the night, never to be seen again.

Thirty years later, an advertisement appears in the local paper of a small town in California. A lady marks the paper as she drinks her coffee. She moves to the phone booth to call the number, glancing at the paper. She smiles as she replaces the receiver and makes her way down the High Street. The middle-aged lady, a good-looking blonde, knocks on the door of the Catholic rectory in answer to the advertised vacancy for a housemaid. She is shown into the lounge and sits waiting for the head priest to arrive to interview her for the position.

Her mind wanders back to the time when she was thirteen years of age. Her father had died, and to help her family she sang in the streets of 'Battle Creek' Michigan. Her blonde hair dangled over her pretty blue eyes and with her sheer power and high spirits she had no trouble in attracting an audience. She bellowed out all the favourite songs of the day. The audiences loved her and everyone knew she had a rare talent. Betty June Thornbury was soon attracting the crowds as she performed on bandstands up and down the country, her exuberance attracting an ever- wider audience as they flocked to the dance halls to watch the girl the papers were calling The Blonde Bombshell. Her name was getting top-billing in front of the bands and theatres and dance halls were queuing up to get an engagement. They all wanted a piece of the action – and when Betty appeared you did get action.

Hollywood was beginning to take notice and, in 1942, she made her film debut in *The Fleets In*. By 1947 her film career had already taken off with two successful biopics, *Incendiary Blonde* based on the life of Texas

Guinan and *The Perils of Pauline*, the life story of the silent-screen star Pearl White. She is best remembered from when she took over the role of the tough but vulnerable Annie in *Annie Get Your Gun* from the ailing Judy Garland.

Betty had arrived and was at the top of the ladder in Hollywood. The scripts were piling in and even Fred Astaire partnered her in *Let's Dance* in 1950. Here was a star who not only could sing, but could act as well, as in *The Miracle of Morgan's Creek*. Now she was dancing with Fred Astaire and to do this you had to be good. Cecil B de Mille had also noticed her talent and gave her the lead in the star-studded circus epic *The Greatest Show on Earth* in 1952. More films followed and she played a vaudeville star in *Somebody Loves Me* but, in 1957, *Spring Reunion* was her last film. She walked out on her contract because the studio refused to let her then husband direct the movie. She walked into the wilderness and became a recluse. No one knew what had happened to her and several rumours circulated over the years. When they stopped, she was just another forgotten star.

The middle aged lady's mind returns to the lounge of the priest's house as the head priest enters to interview her.

"So, you would like to join us here at the rectory, would you Miss … Miss …?"

"Thornbury." answers Betty. The priest looks at her "I seem to know your face."

"Yes" replies Betty, "I used to be in films."

"Of course" says the priest, "It's Betty Hutton!"

The small boy cries out in the night, his cries turning into screams. Young David's parents run into his room to comfort the toddler who has just woken from yet another bad dream. His mother's embrace quickly soothes his fears and he is smiling again as Daddy carries him on his back to their room. Young David was born in 1930 and his parents, like many of that time, wanted their child to be in films. So many child stars were coming to the forefront during the Thirties. Queues of mothers with crying kids stretched for hundreds of yards outside the film studios. Each mother thought their child was going to be the next Jackie Cooper, Margaret O'Brien or Mickey Rooney. David was one of these kids, but one of the unfortunate ones who were left in the crowd, only to be included as an extra in many of the wartime films. During this time David went through spasms of bad dreams that woke him up in a cold sweat. On a number of occasions his dreams reflected true-life happenings and sometimes they were like premonitions. He was always a deep thinker, never much of a smiler, maybe his solemn appearance held him back from being a child star. One can appreciate that his worried look was attributable to those bad dreams and the fact that he must have tried to stay awake, frightened to go to sleep.

In 1945, he got a better break in films with his first speaking part in *It's a Pleasure*, starring the skating star Sonja Henie. Bit-parts followed in a number of pictures that included *Bonzo goes to College* in 1955. The films came and went just like the bad dreams but now TV was becoming more popular and cinema audiences dwindled. David's good looks had developed and he was sought after by a number of studios. There were plenty of half hour TV series that ranged from Westerns and crime to comedy. Studios were churning out these mini-spectaculars like confetti and David was suited to many of these roles, except the comedy ones – he found it hard to smile. He was by now in his early thirties and his dreams were as explicit as ever. He had thought that now he was in demand more than ever before, his dreams might ease off but that was not to be. The strain from lack of sleep still showed in his slow style of acting. He realised that he was becoming popular and was being recognised in the street, which made him happy enough but in his dreams he was running away from something or somebody and he would get up, have a drink and ponder why he was running – running to where or from whom?

Six months later, the studio called him into the producer's office to offer him his biggest breakthrough to date.

"David, we have a great part for you. It could go on for three years. The scripts will suit you down to the ground. The story line is that you are convicted of the murder of your wife. You plead your innocence, claiming that you saw the murderer, a man with one arm, running away. You escape when the train that is transporting you to the penitentiary is derailed and you are on the run for the three-year series." David Jansson is rooted to the spot, unable to speak.

"David, are you all right? What do you think of the story? Each week the scripts will have different guest stars. It will be called *The Fugitive*."

David Jansson was running, as in his dreams, for the next four years. His dreams were different now, but still bad enough to wake him up. He emerged as a big star with *The Fugitive* being shown in over eighty countries throughout the world. Coincidentally, one of his big movies in later years was called *Nowhere to Run*. Other series which proved successful were *Harry O* which ran for three years and *The Golden Gate Murders* in 1980.

Throughout the *Golden Gate Murders* series, David's sleep is disturbed by the usual cold sweats. He is very concerned over the real-life coincidences that have already taken place. After a hard day's work, sleep is hard to fight off. He drifts off into a dream … crowds have gathered outside a house and he stands amongst the onlookers as a coffin is brought out through the doorway and carried to a hearse. David, still in his dream, asks a bystander who the dead person was. The man turns to him and says "Some actor by the name of Jansson!" He awoke, terror-stricken. Disturbed by the dream he goes for an urgent medical check-up and was assured that all was well. Forty eight hours after the dream he dies of a heart attack! He is only fifty years-old.

The Fugitive, who captured all our hearts in the Sixties, was now dead. Dreams had played a major part in the star's life – but now the nightmare was over!

The one-time Hollywood heart-throb sits in the lounge of his ranch house. He is feeling very depressed as he downs yet another drink. The puffiness in his face is taking away the sharp, distinguished good looks which made his female fans scream and swoon when his face appeared on the screen. Although his face has lost its youthful, handsome appearance, he is still an attractive man. His hair is still blonde as it flops over his blue eyes. His small frame looks lost in the extra-large lounge chair. The bottle is half-empty. It is well known throughout the movie world that he has a drink problem. He sits in despair and reminisces over his days of stardom. Tonight is no different to any other night. It is the same chair in the same lounge, the only thing that is different is the bottle.

This ex-heartthrob was born in Hot Springs, Arkansas, his family moving to California while he was still a child. He was a great athlete and won medals for diving. Because of his fitness and good looks he was soon noticed by the Hollywood scouts. Universal Studios put him into many B pictures and he also worked in radio between film castings. Universal Studios loved his looks but wished he was taller. He remained a bit-part player for years, one of these parts being one of the many reporters in the last scene of Orson Welles' *Citizen Kane*. He removed the pipe from his mouth to say the two words "Oh! Rosebud" and that was another picture over.

He was just getting by, scraping a living and on the whole feeling very miserable because he had not made a success in films. To make matters worse, his mother committed suicide in 1937. With his lack of success as well as height he was about to give it all up – but which road should he take? The way of his mother or go back east?

The depression has really got a hold on him as he empties the bottle and falls asleep. The siren of an ambulance breaks the silence of the woodlands surrounding the ranch. Alan Ladd is rushed to hospital with gunshot wounds to his chest. These were self-inflicted, from his shotgun, apparently as he went in pursuit of a prowler, although no evidence was found of any disturbance at the ranch-house. As he is nursed back to health, he has more time to reminisce on his past career. He lies back on the many pillows piled behind him and his thoughts drift to Sue Carol, an ex-actress who opened an agency. She took to Alan and saw he had potential.

"Let's get some built-up shoes and make that five foot-six into five foot-nine" she suggested. Sue Carol organised the right kind of photographs and it was "Paramount here I come." Sue and Alan were married and she concentrated more on Alan's future than the rest of her agency's business. His first success was a film called *Joan of Paris* with Paul Henreid and Thomas Mitchell, a war propaganda film with Alan at the bottom of the main cast. He did not stay at the bottom for long, Paramount gave him the lead, co-starring with Veronica Lake in *This Gun for Hire*. He played the hired gun, a ruthless killer whose cold, sultry looks sent the female fans wild. This was followed by another film with Veronica Lake, *The Glass Key*. Alan Ladd was up there at the top. Although he never got on with Lake, he made another picture with her, *The Blue Dahlia*, in 1946. Ladd made some good films in the Forties, *Two Years before the Mast*, *Calcutta* and *The Great Gatsby*.

The young nurse fixes his pillows as he tries to get ease from the pain of his wounds. He thinks of Sue and appreciates how her perseverance brought him stardom. If only he could live those Forties again! After several weeks in hospital Alan goes home to be depressed once again and back to the bottle and the home movies, the large chair and the loneliness. He plays his copy of *The Great Gatsby*. He knows the films which followed it were not up to standard. At the beginning of the Fifties, Paramount gave him the mediocre pictures *Branded* and *Red Mountain*. Paramount was not impressed with the result and about to part company with the former bit-part player when up pops the script of one of the best classic Westerns ever to hit the silver screen – it still gets a four-star rating when it appears each year on our small screens. *Shane* saves the day for Alan Ladd and he is up there once again with the stars. *Shane* was a budget film with a small cast and an even smaller town. It became a big hit and, if ever a picture needed a sequel this was it. It should have kept Alan on the right road, at the top but he carried on along an avenue of ordinary films. His last film, *The Carpetbaggers*, had a good script and a bit of meat in his last fight when he gave George Peppard a good hiding.

The bottle again is half-empty and he thinks of the roles that were offered to him but which he could not take because of the booze. *Giant*, which was eventually given to James Dean, was one of them.

Alan Ladd was a little, big man. His five foot six-inches and three-inch shoes made those stories about standing on a box pure fallacy. His deep voice and his looks gave him one of the largest fan clubs of any Hollywood star. His photograph, the property of my sister, was framed on my family's sideboard. She, like millions of women, thought he was the biggest star ever to come out of Hollywood. The bottle is empty now as he lies back in his chair but this time beside the bottle there is an empty sleeping-tablet box. Goodbye Shane!

He became one of the richest men in America, although he had started out as a straight actor. Hollywood in 1920 was full of actors looking for work so Harold Lloyd had to change his image. He took film-extra work, hoping that his chance might come through some other avenue. It did when, by chance, he made Hal Roach laugh. This gave Harold an opening in comedy-shorts, playing a character by the name of Lonesome Luke. This did not work as well as the actor would have liked. He felt that he needed a recognisable trademark. Chaplin had the bowler and cane, Keaton had that solemn face … but no-one wore glasses. Yes, Harold Lloyd, the bespectacled comedian, took off, making more films than Chaplin and Keaton put together.

He became known as the Third Genius. His daredevil escapades included hanging from planks from half-finished skyscrapers and he had been near to death on many occasions while doing his own stunts. In one scene, a live bomb went off prematurely and he lost a thumb and finger as well as sustaining facial injuries. His hospitalisation brought flowers and get-well cards from all over the world. He was now challenging Chaplin for supremacy at the box office. He was directing his directors, making full-length films and hit followed hit. His daring stunts brought hysteria to audiences. The trick photography that was used was so life-like that audiences were screaming with fright. People fainted and ambulances were on call to cinemas where Harold was featuring. This played havoc with hospital schedules and they tried to ban some of his films. It was decided to bring in first aid to assist with the casualties, keeping the ambulances free to be on call for more urgent emergency treatment.

Hal Roach and Harold Lloyd produced eight years of silent comedy. They are now in the archives with the best of the classics. Harold then moved on to producing and brought us another type of comedy which featured a gang of boys and girls who were always full of mischief and who gave us joy and sorrow; those lovable youngsters – *Our Gang*. The comic genius had overcome many obstacles since his teenage acting-days but now another innovation comes to the surface. Comedy was no longer 'in', it was sound, voices, singing. Al Jolson's *Jazz Singer* had set the world alight and studios had to be revamped. Some went bankrupt but Harold came up trumps once again when his public wanted to hear him talk. When they did, they laughed as usual.

Gradually, good story-lines became scarce. One script was financed by the great Howard Hughes, who broke Harold's heart with the amount of cutting that was done to the film. Harold retired, having been the most successful artiste to convert from silent to sound films. He came out of retirement to supervise a compilation of his greatest scenes, winning the Palme D'Or at the Cannes Film Festival. Harold died of cancer in 1971, aged seventy seven. They say silence is golden. To his fans, the name of Harold Lloyd is!

One of the biggest love stories in show business was that of a couple who loved one another till the day they died. They married and divorced twice and although they were apart in their latter years, their love for each other endured. He once had the best Latin American band in the States and his Cuban looks made him a real Don Juan. He dated all the beauties of the day, Betty Grable, Lana Turner, Ann Miller. Females flocked around him in droves. Desi Arnez was the toast of New York, appearing at all the best night clubs. The Latin sound was in and when Desi played the congo drum the fans went wild.

One of Desi's shows was so successful that RKO film studios wanted to take it to Hollywood as a movie. On the set of that film was a pretty blonde with big blue eyes. Desi spotted her and asked her name. "Lucille" she replied. He replied "I love Lucy!" Being a romeo with a reputation, Lucille ignored him and Desi returned to New York after the film was made and Lucille carried on making her contract films with RKO. But love had struck both of them – they met again and got married. The press made a big thing of Desi's one night stands – and they did not mean on the band stands! Sometimes he would gamble all the band's earnings in one night in Las Vegas casinos.

Their marriage was dissolved but their love was still strong. They wrote to each other over a long period. Desi's coach crashed on his way to see Lucille in her show: many were killed but Desi escaped injury. They married again and decided to try and work together in films. RKO refused so they tried television companies. Television did not like the idea either so they went on stage to prove to everyone that it would work. The public loved the show so, eventually, a one-off pilot television programme was made.

But something was missing – the audience. Lucille worked better with a live audience but a studio set which could hold an audience would cost an extra five thousand dollars per show. The two big parties in the production refused to put up the extra money. Desi offered to pay the extra on condition that he would keep the film rights. It was agreed. Desi

Arnez had turned television around, that is how live TV audiences were born. Other studios brought in canned laughter which was never as successful.

Two children and many years of happiness later they still loved working together. They were workaholics but at least it kept the marriage on the right wavelength. *I Love Lucy* was such a success. The productions were by then called Desilu. It wasn't long before they bought out RKO studios, where other films were made. They were America's best loved couple, their productions were being televised in sixty countries. Their empire now caused quarrels and, sadly, they were divorced again. Lucy continued with the show, renaming it *The Lucy Show*. They were again apart and wrote of their love to one another until Desi died aged sixty nine. Lucille was heartbroken and suffered until she died aged seventy seven, with all those letters still intact.

The big band sound has a great following today and although you do not hear any in the Hit Parade, the music of yesteryear is certainly big business in the CD world. There are over two hundred big bands registered in the UK and that takes a lot of following. Thousands of fans attend the big band concerts and festivals that take place up and down the country every week of the year. No matter which big band is on stage, whether it be Andy Prior, Chris Dean, Ken McIntosh, the Squadronaires, the BBC Dance Orchestra or Sid Laurence, you can be sure a Glenn Miller arrangement is in their repertoire.

Glenn was an ambitious trombone player. He had been doing pretty well for himself as a session player with several bands and as an organiser and arranger of the Ray Noble Orchestra. Although he was also one of the top trombonists in the New York Radio Station and recording studios, he wanted his own band, so he set about putting one together. Musically it was quite good, but it failed to make the mark. He was doing a lot of freelance work and was one of the best session men in New York. He was forever trying new ideas in his arrangements, persuading the big names in the business to try them out but they were handed back. "Keep to the standard arrangements, Glenn" he was told over and over again. "Stop trying to change what everybody wants." So it was back to the baton, still looking for the sound that kept on haunting him.

His band broke up from lack of funds and his trombone made regular appearances in the pawnbroker's window. His determination got the better of him and, after many sleepless nights, the trombone was back polished, ready to form a quartet, adding a bit more sound, making it a quintet – a sextet was just around the corner and when a couple of future big names, Tex Bencke and Wilbur Schwartz, liked what they heard they brought it to an eight-piece.

Auditions and countless practice nights brought trouble. Glenn was a perfectionist and many a musician was replaced by the strict trombone player. He was not the easy-going Mr Nice Guy that James Stewart's portrayal in Glenn's life story would lead you to believe. By now, Glenn had seventeen musicians under his baton, including four trombones, four trumpets, five saxaphones. Different brass sections replaced others in numerous permutations until, finally, everything gelled; Glenn had found his new sound. All it needed was a bit of polish and a few dance hall gigs to bring it to perfection.

The youngsters went wild with the sound. The press took notice. On his birthday, 1 March 1939, he opened at the Glenn Island Casino in New York, the same club that had launched the Dorsey Brothers and many successful, named bands. By the end of 1940, the Glenn Miller Orchestra was the country's number one dance band. When America joined the war, Glenn applied for an air force commission and built the greatest dance band of all time for that service. He took it to Europe, playing for millions of G.I.s, both in person and on the radio. In December 1944, on what was to have been a routine flight from France to England, Glenn Miller was lost and his aircraft was never traced.

That is not quite the end of this profile because recently we are being told of various possibilities to Glenn Millers end. One story says that he never got on the plane. One witness has now come forward to say that she was with Glenn four days after he had been reported missing. Another version is that the plane went on a spying mission and that he was captured behind enemy lines, the plane never setting off for England. Whatever happened, we know that Glenn did not arrive in this country. But his music did and his British fans have been In the Mood ever since!

Dr **Wendell Mitchell,** the Universal Studios physician, is sent for in order to attend to two of Universal's stars – Angela Lansbury and Robert Falk. An outbreak of food poisoning was affecting their two productions, *Columbo* and *Murder She Wrote*. The two screen detectives lay in their beds feeling very sick but this time they were unable to tell who had done it. Possibly the cause was outside caterers or the studio canteen. Did they both visit the same restaurant in Beverley Hills? An unlikely option as there are twenty thousand of them serving the elite of show business.

Dr Mitchell cannot be found. He should have reported back from holiday the day before so a second doctor is brought in from the local hospital and he immediately admits Falk and Lansbury to private wards. A thorough examination is made of all catering facilities and of all the production team. Treatment with appropriate medication is given and within a week or so the studio is back in full swing, with Columbo scratching his head. But where was Dr Wendell Mitchell. He had still not returned from holiday in Canada. He was a single man so there was some concern about him not informing Universal of his whereabouts. Personnel carried out an investigation through the travel agencies, airports and railway stations and concluded that although his destination had been Canada, no hotels had played host to the physician. The field narrowed down to Lynhurst Cottage. The agent for the cottage told James Cannon, Universal Studios Personnel Manager, that Dr Mitchell had had a breakdown and was in Ridgeley Hospital, under the supervision of Dr Madeley. What had caused his breakdown? Dr Mitchell was able to relate the following in his own words.

"I came to Lynhurst Cottage a month ago for peace and tranquillity. It was good to get away from the hubbub of the studios and a city which travels at a hundred miles an hour. I needed to slow down and felt that the cottage would bring me back to reality. You get a lot of snow here, so the comfort of the cottage gives complete rest. At the end of the first week, on the Saturday night, it was near bedtime and I wanted to finish the chapter of the book I was reading. My eyes were heavy and I must have closed them for a moment. I opened them suddenly because of a loud but slow knocking at the door. The snow was collecting quite quickly on the outside panes and I thought that it must be someone wanting shelter from the storm. The knocking became louder but was just as slow. I unbolted the door. The snowstorm forced the door out of my grip, turning the hall into a winter scene. Standing on the doorstep was a child of about nine years-old.

"Dr Mitchell, my Mummy is sick, will you come with me?" she said.

"Come in my child, while I get dressed" I replied, but the child stayed where she was.

"Come quick, please" she pleaded. I quickly dressed for the journey while she remained standing on the doorstep. She was wearing a well-worn blue dress which was partly ripped and her shoes had seen better days. She had no top coat or head covering.

"Put this coat over your head, child" I said but the little girl took no heed and merely turned and walked down the path. I followed quickly. The snow was so heavy that it was difficult at times to see the little girl ahead who sometimes disappeared completely only to re-appear at my side to take my hand as we fought against the driving snow. I tried to shelter the child from the winter blizzard as we trudged on to the girl's house and I was exhausted. "How much further," I thought.

A light flickered in the distance, we were there at last! The home was of poor quality and my footsteps echoed on the uncovered stairs as I ascended towards the landing light. The bedroom door was open and I could see that the lady in the bed was ill. During my examination she said "Thank you, Dr Mitchell, how did you know that I was ill?"

"Never mind" I replied "Just get some sleep."

I stayed all night. Eventually the lady's temperature dropped to a safe level and she was able to talk. I asked her how she knew my name. She replied "I used to work for you many years ago in your reception and have always spoken highly of you." Then I remembered her as one of my employees from twenty years ago. She sat up and took a little soup.

"Tell me" she said "How did you know that I was sick?"

Obviously she was still not herself, I thought and answered, "Why, your courageous little girl braved the elements to bring me here through the snow storm. How she found me I do not know because I am only here on holiday and I have only seen two people in the last week."

The lady looked shocked. "What little girl?" she replied.

Yes, I began to think, what little girl? I had not seen the child since arriving at the house the night before.

"Your little girl," I continued "She asked me to come to her Mummy quickly as she was ill. She was wearing very few clothes, in fact only a skimpy, blue dress."

Tears filled the lady's eyes. "But my little girl died two months ago, the only clothes she had are hanging up over there."

I looked over to where the lady was pointing and saw a dress, a blue dress with two rips in it, just as I had seen the night before on the little girl. What mysterious influence had brought that girl to me? My mind is blank, as if the curtain has been drawn at the end of another Hollywood script."

The queues for the cinema in the 1930s and 1940s brought the busiest two decades the cinema has ever known in its one hundred years. The queues created work for the busker who went from one cinema to another, passing his collection box or battered hat in front of the cinema-goers. Sometimes you gave, sometimes you didn't, depending on what mood the busker's entertainment had inspired. Whether you gave or not was irrelevant to the admission fee for the cinema. What you did not realise was that a percentage of the price of the ticket was going to the mob in Chicago. This is how it all started.

Prohibition had finished in America and the gangs were looking for new avenues to make money. A run-down ex-bootlegger was paying one of his regular visits to one of the many soup-kitchens that occupied the streets of many American cities in those depression years. His name was Willie Byoff. He met George Browne, a small-time union official of the cinema, giving a hand to feed out-of-work diners, many of them ex-cinema and theatre workers. Word was out that cutbacks were about to take place in the larger cinemas and theatres that would leave only one person to operate the projection booths. The ex-bootlegger convinced the union official to advise Paramount Circuit that they would organise a strike if these cutbacks happened. Paramount responded with a gesture of a one hundred and fifty dollar a week donation towards the soup kitchen. This wasn't good enough for the ex-bootlegger, who said "Now that we are talking money, let's say fifty thousand dollars." Twenty thousand dollars was the compromise and that was the start of the cinema protection racket.

The twenty thousand dollar bribe was like the ring of a cash register to the ears of the Chicago mob which was led by Frank Nitty, now that Al Capone was in jail. The mob immediately contacted Byoff and Browne and told them, "We will be taking over the unions with your help. Of course, of all the money coming your way, fifty per cent will be ploughed into the organisation." Browne, with the help of the mob, became president of the Chicago cinema union. All those who objected to this were persuaded by the mob to stand down, or else. Paramount Circuit Cinemas soon showed their displeasure about the extortionate demands imposed on them. but when every projectionist switched off his machine at 8pm on November 30 1935, leaving audiences without a show, the studios realised just how powerful the IATSE union had become. Their cinemas lay empty as strikes all over Chicago were organised. This caused a cashflow problem and work at the film studios came to a halt. Redundancies followed, making more people than ever out of work in an already depressed America.

The IATSE union (IA for short) was now the biggest theatrical union in America and the studios bowed to the union's wishes. Even in the credits before and after a picture you will see the logo IA credited to the film. Paramount became a closed shop and every position right down to the usherette in the smallest of cinemas was under the rule of the Mob. Browne had become the president of the union nationwide, with Byoff making the blueprints for the millions of dollars that were rolling in. Of course, there was the fifty per cent going to Frank Nitty and company, who provided five minders each for Byoff and Browne. They had come a long way since that day in the soup kitchen!

New York was their next stop. What had happened in Chicago was to be offered to the big film bosses who were resident in the Big Apple. All Hollywood decisions were made there and Warner Brothers, RKO, Universal and MGM were now in the web. Byoff and Browne's motto to the moguls was "Shut up, put up, or get out" Byoff's greed was really showing as he was now trying to buy the actors' union, starting with the extras. This upset the main actors because they knew that this would be the thin end of the wedge. A lot of publicity was appearing in the press which made many of the studios feel uneasy, especially Twentieth Century Fox. They footed the bill for Byoff and his wife to take a world cruise on the Queen Mary. Champagne and orchids were sent aboard, courtesy of Warner Brothers. Accompanying them on the trip was Mrs Louis B Mayer.

In the meantime a couple of union dissidents decided to employ a private investigator to delve into Byoff's and Browne's backgrounds. At the same time, one of the main actors of the day, Robert Montgomery, representing the Hollywood actors and using his own money, started an investigation of the crooked pair. It proved worthwhile as both were brought before a Grand Jury and received ten year sentences. While in jail, Byoff decided to talk of their association with the Mob. Their evidence convicted the Mob, which included Johnnie Roselli, Louis Compania, Charlie Joy, Paul Reeka and Frank Nitty. Nitty could not face the music. He made his way to a disused railway siding, fired two shots into the air to attract attention, and then shot himself.

The remainder of the mob were also sentenced to ten years each. A couple of them got out after three years. They went to the Reverie Hotel, Las Vegas and planned the downfall of Byoff, who had got off with a light sentence. (Browne died after his release in June 1956, never having worked again). Leaving his home to go on a fishing trip, Byoff turned on the ignition of his car. The car exploded into small pieces of shrapnel and parts of Willie Byoff's body were not much bigger. When the police arrived, Mrs Byoff was on a step ladder screaming as she looked through the tall bushes. The police, thinking she had gone crazy, tried to console her as she screamed "I must find it, I must find it." It turned out that she was looking for one of Willie's fingers which was wearing a very large diamond ring!

Willie Byoff's claim had been that he was the King of Hollywood and that the film bosses danced to his music. Was this the music that the little busker played as we queued to pay our admission fee?

The Hollywood jeweller closes for the night. The staff make certain that all the precious rings and stones are locked away in the safe and that all the expensive gifts are secured in the cabinets. The glass corner-cabinet displays costume jewellery and other not so expensive items. On the top shelf there is a not very attractive, heavy, metal ring which features a large but dull stone. Why was it there? What was it doing in such an attractive shop in Beverley Hills? The ring stood out like a sore thumb. Who would buy it? It would look more at home on a battered metal tray in a junk shop window. but there is something about this finger-band as it lies on the top corner-shelf. As the staff do their last chores of the night, the dull stone of the ring reflects the light, giving the impression of an eye, wandering from one end of the shop to the other. The staff say their goodnights to one another, leaving the shop owner to his end of the day paper work.

The jeweller's shop has been in the owner's family for the best part of the century. The jeweller enters the date in his book and as he glances around the shop the reflection from the stone in the ring catches his eye. It should have sent a shiver down his spine but by now he was used to its strange, mysterious and deadly powers. The jeweller looks at the date again and his mind wanders back to 1920 and to the story that he was told by his grandfather. The family's other jewellery store in San Francisco was rather busy that day for a side-street store. The owner was rather surprised to see a celebrity in the shop and offered him immediate assistance.

"I am interested in the silver ring in the window," said the film star.

"Yes, certainly, Mr Valentino," replied the jeweller. The other customers in the shop could not believe their eyes as they looked at the great Rudolph Valentino. The owner brought the tray of rings from the window. After signing a few autographs, the star listened to the jeweller.

"I would not like you to buy this ring, sir. It does not have a pleasant history!"

"It appeals to me and I must have it." Valentino insisted. "I was walking past your store when it caught my eye and drew me into your shop. I tell you I must have it."

Reluctantly the jeweller parted with the ring, Mr Valentino ignoring the jeweller's advice about the curse. Rudolph looked forward to the pleasure of showing his friends the ring with the evil history. His studio urged him to wear the ring in his next film *The Young Rajah* – the film was his first flop. Rudolph did not blame the ring for the failure of the film but his friends encouraged him to get rid of it. He wore it in his next and last film *The Son of the Sheik*. He was still wearing it when he went on holiday to New York and as he lay in the morgue, after dying of acute appendicitis.

Pola Nigre, a 1920s film starlet whose career was now taking off, was a friend of Rudolph. The ring was given to her – she became ill and was unable to work for twelve months. When she eventually recovered and auditioned for work, the studio turned her down. Although she too did not blame the ring, she decided to get rid of it. At a party, she noticed a young band-singer who had the sharp, Latin looks of Valentino. She requested a song and gave him the ring. The young singer was Russ Columbo and great things were expected of this talented songster. Columbo wore the ring but not for long as he died in a shooting accident three weeks later.

The ring had now gravitated to the ownership of Joe Casino, a friend of Columbo. Casino had unhappy vibrations from the ring and put it into a glass case. When he was invited to one of the big annual parties in the area, he thought "I'll wear the ring." He died a week later in a traffic accident as he was returning from the party. Although he was wearing the ring when he died, it was not buried with him. Joe's brother Del, who had laughed at the idea of a ring with a curse on it had said "Give it to me, I'll wear it. You have to laugh at these things in the face." He wore it for some time. Had he beaten the curse? It certainly seemed that way. Del Casino kept the ring in a safe at his home. When a burglar broke into his home the alarm bell brought the police cars screaming to the Casino home. The silhouette of the burglar was caught in the beam of the police lights. A shot was fired and the thief, James Willis, was killed. In his possession was the Valentino ring! The ring was put back in the safe where it stayed, out of harm's way.

Producer Edward Small decided to make a film about Rudolph Valentino. A look-alike was searched for nationally. A twenty two year old skater by the name of Jack Dunn was cast to play Valentino. The producer borrowed the ring from Del Casino to make the film more authentic. The test was a great success and the picture was scheduled to commence in two weeks. But, ten days after Jack Dunn's screen test, he died from a rare blood disease. Del Casino reclaimed the ring vowing that no-one would ever wear it again. It was put into a safety deposit box in a Los Angeles bank but even the steel walls of the bank could not provide protection; an earthquake and an explosion raised the bank to the ground, scattering fragments from the deposit boxes.

Some years later, a down-and-out character called into a jewellers shop with a ring. The jeweller recognised the soil-ingrained finger-band as the Valentino ring. After the transaction was completed, the jeweller performed his restoration skills on the silver piece and placed it in the display cabinet, ready to be shown to the customers of Beverley Hills.

The owner remembers the story so vividly as he puts his books away for the evening. The stone in the ring catches his eye once more as he turns out the lights …

The tough, little guy of Hollywood finishes another day on the set. He sits in his dressing room with his head in his hands, not wanting to go home to the wife he loves so very much. Gladys suffers from depression, loving her husband one minute and despising him the next so that he never knows what will face him when he returns at the end of the day.

His close associates at the film studios begged him to finish the marriage, as it was affecting his acting which meant longer hours on the set and more retakes. His popularity began to wane, and the up-and-coming Humphrey Bogart took over as Hollywood's leading gangster. "I can't leave her" he would say, "I love her so much, what would happen to her?" His eyes would fill with tears as he opened his heart to colleagues and anyone who would listen to his heartbreaking situation. No-one would dream that the little, tough guy Edward G Robinson, the Little Caesar of Hollywood, needed a shoulder to cry on.

He was born Emmanuel Goldberg and, like many of the great actors of the time, found fame on the Broadway stage. In 1925, he met Gladys Lloyd. He loved her from the moment he saw her but she displayed a love/hate relationship right from the start. It was two years before they married and Edward G always thought that someday she would change. He doted on her, giving her anything she wanted and finding her acting work in order to be closer to her. They moved to Hollywood in 1929 where he was an instant hit in *Little Caesar*, a name which stuck with him throughout his career. Gladys took to the life of luxury, the parties, the swimming pools and the hospitality as if she were born to it. In his heyday, Edward G bought a mock-tudor mansion and turned the badminton court into an art gallery. This was to become one of the finest art collections in America. He loved his collection but it was only his second love, he still idolised Gladys and nothing was too much trouble to make her happy. If he was away for an hour, he would phone her to make sure that she was all right. He was always afraid that the depression she had once suffered would return. His fanatical love for her was so obvious to his fellow artistes who said that he loved her too much. Then, slowly but surely the dreaded depression returned. The Hollywood style of living began to get on her nerves. She started to throw tantrums and her rapid mood changes meant life for the Robinsons was becoming impossible. Nothing that Edward G did eased the situation and his gifts were thrown back at him as he reiterated his love for her. He tried to provide her with the best clinical treatment but was accused of trying to get rid of her! The following day she would beg his forgiveness but then the next day another gift would be violently rejected! Their friends now stayed away from the vast mansion as Gladys's behaviour was intolerable.

Edward G would come down from his bedroom in the middle of the night to sit amongst his art collection as this was his only comfort and relief from his beautiful but neurotic wife. He shed silent tears, murmuring "I loved you when I first saw you, I love you now and I will always love you." One night Edward G sat looking at his art collection, knowing that it was to be sold the next day, along with the mansion, so that he could give half of everything he had to Gladys. He had lost his first love and was now parting with his second, in an attempt to regain the first.

When Gladys died he was able to buy back some of that collection. As he sat in the peace and tranquillity of his old age, looking at the old masters, his thoughts were never very far from his Gladys.

Edward G died in 1973. He was buried, as he had wished, by the side of the woman on whom he had lavished so much love and in return received so much torment.

It is 1934 and a small picture house is showing the star-studded movie *Manhattan Melodrama*. Though this picture is only an average production, it achieves worldwide fame because sitting in the audience that evening is none other than John Dillenger. Sitting with him is the famous Lady in Red who has set Dillenger up to meet his end by being shot down outside the picture-house. One of the young actors, who plays a boy from the slums in the movie, benefits because the movie attracts more publicity. Yes, one of those slum boys is Mickey Rooney.

Born in 1920, Mickey was christened Joe Yule. As the son of a vaudeville comedian, he had his first taste of the stage when he crawled onto it from his buggy in the wings as his mum and dad performed their act. He was only eighteen months old but the applause made him star-struck. From then on he was included as part of the act, pushing his dad out of the star spot. His parents were divorced by the time he was three and Mrs Yule brought up little Joey alone. She knew he had talent and took him to Hollywood where they were auditioning for *Our Gang*. Joey could have had a part as one of the gang but Mrs Yule wanted a better part (and a better salary) for her talented son. She returned home to bide her time. She knew that the movie-makers had noticed Joey's rare talent and that he would to be the next big child star. Back in Hollywood, he got a few bit parts with small film companies.

When Mrs Yule heard through her agent that Louis Meyer was looking for a dark-haired kid to play Mickey McGuire, (a part adapted from a cartoon character), she dyed Mickey's hair. He got the part and become one of the biggest stars MGM ever produced. He played the part of McGuire for the next six years. Joey adopted the cartoon character's Christian name and Mickey Rooney was born.

His big break came with *Manhattan Melodrama*. The John Dillinger shoot-out had given this picture more free advertising through press reports than any other movie in Hollywood's history. It became a smash hit, mainly due to the film-goers curiosity.

Throughout the Thirties, Mickey starred with all the big names and always "stole the picture". By the end of the decade, he was the most famous teenager in America and the cockiest kid in Hollywood. A series of Andy Hardy films were next and when, in 1939, Hollywood produced more classic movies in one year than ever before or since with *Gone with the Wind, Stagecoach, The Wizard of Oz* - who was the biggest star? Yes, Mickey Rooney, whose films had grossed over thirty million dollars in that year alone. But Mickey was only on half the salary of the other top stars because he was only nineteen. He had the best of everything and was travelling in the fast lane, wining and dining the most beautiful women in town.

Mickey then teamed up with Judy Garland, toppling Fred Astaire and Ginger Rogers as the top dance team. He was big box office, bigger than Gable or Garbo. He attracted the raven beauty, Ava Gardner and entered into the first of his marriages but it only lasted for nine months, due to his jealousy. Army service gave Mickey the rank of sergeant and a second marriage brought two children. He then met and married Martha Vickers but this soon ended to make way for Elaine Makin, a beauty queen and Mrs Rooney number four.

Television played its part in Mickey's downfall, as he appeared in a couple of flops. The future Mrs Rooney number five was five months pregnant by the time divorce came through. Many actors thought that Mickey shot himself in the foot regarding his career. When he was kicked off a live TV show on which he was a guest, for being abusive, the crowd cheered and applauded. Mickey's fifth wife, Barbara, had given birth to their fourth child. Mickey was still playing around but it was his wife who became caught up in a romance with Milosh, a Czech actor who Mickey had brought back to America after appearing in a movie with him in Europe. Mickey ended up in hospital with depression and he and Barbara got back together. Tragically, Milosh killed Barbara in a fit of rage before shooting himself with Mickey's own .38 revolver.

His marriage to wife number six, Marsh Lane, lasted just one hundred days, during which time he lost his mother and also his lifelong friend, Judy Garland. He then met Karolyn Harket who was to become wife number seven. Lack of finance proved too much for this marriage. Mickey turned to the theatre but on the first night only fifteen people turned up. It was a beginning. His determination got him more roles and eventually Mickey was again a star, this time on Broadway. Jan Chamberlain became wife number eight.

Again Mickey is big box office. The little big giant of Hollywood believes you only get out of life what you put into it. There is only one you. His autobiography tells it all. Its title? ... *Life's Too Short*.

The clock strikes two am and two loud peels echo around the Civic Centre just outside New York's Manhattan. The restaurant is still busy and several of its customers check their watches with the chimes. Sitting at one of the tables is a distinguished-looking gentleman who is completely bald. He chatters away with his guests, wisecracking at every opportunity and drawing laughter from his three associates. His agent, director and producer have just agreed on the TV detective's next series. Our TV personality sips his brandy and plays with a toothpick.

The foursome carry on with their discussion. Telly Savalas, the bald-headed TV and film star, relaxes over coffee at the end of a successful dinner and business meeting. The time is half past two and Telly decides to call it a night, shaking hands with his guests as he leaves the table. He shakes more hands before he emerges from the restaurant lobby. The commissionaire signals for Mr Savalas's car to be brought to the entrance. Telly takes a left, a right and then motors to Long Island. A full moon shines down on the highway that is deserted except for Telly's car. The rhythm of the engine falters as its power fails. Telly's foot pushes hard down on the accelerator, leaving no space between the floor and the pedal. The car comes to a halt and he tries several times to restart the motor but to no avail. He sinks back into his seat and smacks the palm of his hand against his forehead.

"Of course," he snorts, "the gas!" The fuel gauge points miserably to the bottom of the dial. Telly Savalas tries to make himself comfortable for the remainder of the night but he tosses and turns, trying to ease the numbness in his back. At last he gets into a comfortable position and is just starting to drift off to sleep when the inside of the car is illuminated by the lights of an on-coming vehicle. A car pulls up alongside Telly, who is now sitting upright.

"Are you all right?" asks the stranger.

"Yes," says Telly, "I feel so ashamed, I ran out of gas and I didn't even have a dame with me!"

"Oh! It happens to us all at one time or another, I'll give you a lift to the gas station and bring you back."

"That's very kind of you," replies Telly, getting into the gentleman's black cadillac. Five miles up the highway a petrol station's lights can be seen on the horizon. Telly converses with the bespectacled gentleman during the short journey. A five-gallon can is all that the garage had and it is put into the boot of the Cadillac. Telly makes sure that the immaculately dressed Samaritan with the tight-fitting blue suit does not soil his clothes when trying to give him a hand. Telly suffers another embarrassment when he comes to pay the attendant and finds that he has no money.

"It's all right, Mr Savalas," says the gentleman, passing ten dollars over to the assistant. The Cadillac makes the return journey to Telly's car and the star cannot thank the knight of the road enough for his kindness and consideration.

"Please," insists Telly "Give me your address so that I can repay you." The gentleman is reluctant to do so, saying that it is a pleasure to help such a great star as Kojak but eventually is persuaded to write his address on the back of a business card. Telly thanks him once again and the Cadillac speeds away, leaving Telly to transfer the petrol into his tank. Two days later, Telly sends a nice letter of thanks and a cheque which is more than adequate to cover the gasolene and the inconvenience. A week later a letter arrives at the studios for the attention of Mr Telly Savalas. It is from a Mrs Judith Forsyth and reads:-

"Dear Mr Savalas, I am in receipt of your cheque and letter of the 10th instant. I am deeply grateful for this amount, you are far too generous. My husband John did not tell me about his good deed on the highway. What confuses me about the contents of the letter was the length of time which has passed since your breakdown. My husband died three years ago. Thank you once again for your generosity. Yours sincerely, J Forsyth."

Telly drops into the Director's chair to read the letter over and over again. The next day Telly arrives at Judith Forsyth's house.

"So happy to meet you, Mr Savalas, would you like a nice cup of tea, you look as if you need one, or would you like something stronger?"

"A drop of brandy would be more than acceptable," replies a white-faced Telly.

"This is my husband," says Mrs Forsyth as she shows Telly a photograph. "As I said, he died three years ago."

Telly sips his brandy. "That is the man who helped me on the highway, he wore a light blue suit."

"Yes, that was his favourite," she replies "He was buried in that suit!"

When I think of some of the bad things to come out of Hollywood I am sickened. The scandals, the sham marriages, the drug parties. The sex orgies that caused the downfall of some of some stars like Fatty Arbuckle. The drug pushers (as Peter Lawford was rumoured to be) that caused heartbreak and devastation, ending the careers of Marilyn Monroe and up-and-coming starlets. The publicity-seeking, so-called stars who went to any lengths to get noticed. The cardboard actors of this world who manage to make a name for themselves because the public are vulnerable to a spicey story.

But where there is bad, you will always find good and when you think of something good, you will think of the fine actors who came to the forefront because of their acting ability. One such actor who springs to mind is James Stewart. He was born in 1908, in a small, friendly town in Indiana that had a population of only five thousand. His family was musical and he played the accordion, while his younger sister played the piano and violin. Their mother played the organ in the local church and their father sang in the choir. When not in church or enjoying themselves musically, they worked in the family hardware store.

Jimmy graduated as an architect. While at university he appeared in a university play and caught the acting bug, which led to him getting small parts on Broadway. It was not long before MGM took notice and gave him a seven-year contract worth three hundred and fifty dollars a week. His big break came in 1939 with the film *Mr Smith Goes To Washington*. It was a great success and earned him an Oscar nomination but was beaten to the Oscar by Robert Donat in *Goodbye Mr Chips*. By now, James Stewart was big box office and he cemented his popularity by winning an Oscar in 1940 with *The Philadelphia Story*.

With war looming, Jimmy was off overseas, carrying on the Stewart family tradition of having a serviceman in every American war since the War of Independence. He returned to Hollywood in 1946 with another smash hit *It's a Wonderful Life*. This film is repeatedly shown on television with a five-star rating. James Stewart could do no wrong, he had the

Midas touch. He was up there with all the leading stars. Ginger Rogers, Olivia De Havilland and Lana Turner were just a few of the beauties of the day to link his arm at many of the Hollywood premiere functions. The media was having a field day with the guessing game – who will become Mrs James Stewart? Hundreds of interviews about his matrimonial plans always ended in that famous Stewart drawl: "I guess I'm still looking!" The papers joked that by the time Jimmy got wed the other stars would be onto their fourth marriages! Jimmy reached the age of forty one and said that when he got married it would only be once and that he would stay married. He kept his word.

He met Gloria McLean, a wealthy socialite whose father was a director of MGM, at a Gary Cooper party. It was love at first sight. He said that she was the woman he had always dreamed of and they were married in 1948 – the Coopers, the Tracys and the Nivens were among the many guest stars. Gloria gave birth to twin girls in 1951 and for ten days she was in intensive care. James showed his love and devotion, never leaving her bedside. Their love for each other was regularly featured in the press and photographs always showed them looking into each other's eyes. Their enduring love was so unusual in Hollywood and the public loved it. The Stewart family travelled everywhere together, even when filming in other countries they were never apart.

Sadly, Gloria died in 1994, after a marriage that lasted forty five years. Jimmy never got over his loss. He reached eighty nine and became a recluse. He was proud of his life, he said and was ready for the final curtain. "I am not afraid of death, I've overstayed my welcome ... I know Gloria and I will be together very soon."

And they were. Jimmy died on 2 July 1997.

The British-born comedy film star sits alone in his flat, thinking of the films he has made and the hundreds of stages he has graced while making people laugh. His rocking-chair is motionless as his mind drifts into a state of amnesia. What was it he was thinking about? He could not remember. Maybe it is time to sleep but it is only afternoon – or is it? What time is it? He doesn't know. He has forgotten how to tell the time. During the Seventies, the dreadful Parkinson's Disease had crept up on him, leaving him alone in this very basic flat – his one-time life of luxury now seeming so long ago. His hand cups his forehead and his fingers spread through the grey hair that sits on top of his thin face. His teeth, with their famous gap, try to grasp the gold cigarette holder. It is a heartbreaking vision of a man who once had only to look, without saying anything, to make audiences laugh. His catch-phrases of, "How do you do?" and "You are an absolute bounder" just bowled them over. His famous grin, showing those gap teeth, became his trademark.

Yes, one of my favourite comedians, Terry Thomas, who specialised in playing British upper-class twits, respected rogues and comic cads. His phrases were forced out through his moustache, gap-teeth and cigarette holder. But he was much more than just a comic, he was a good actor who was appreciated over in America appearing in such classics as *Its a Mad, Mad World*, *Those Magnificent Men in their Flying Machines*, and as Jack Lemon's butler in *How to Murder Your Wife*.

His British successes were *I'm All Right Jack* in 1959 and as the rotter in *School for Scoundrels*. He was a big star with non-British audiences who perceived him to be the typical Englishman. Even in real life, if you met him he would say "How do you do?" As a child I remember him appearing at the Royal Court, a star then from his radio days. It was at the Royal Court that a certain teenager broke into his dressing-room in order to steal his famous cigarette-holder. The Liverpool Echo covered the story. The boy was apprehended and brought to court. For some reason he got off even though offences similar to his carried a Borstal sentence. The theft has always stuck in my mind and I am reminded of it every time I see the gold cigarette holder on the screen. It also came back to me when I read news of Terry's illness and how it had got worse over the years. Was it the fact that the robbery had been committed in Liverpool and was featured in the Echo that had made such an impact on my mind? That must have had some effect. But the main reason was that the teenager who had stolen the gold holder went on to become a Liverpool comedian who also achieved national fame.

The irony of all this is that when Terry Thomas's illness worsened to the point when he was dying, the Drury Lane Theatre in London put on a spectacular show of stars who had appreciated Terry. There was sadness in my heart as I thought of the aged comedian, sitting pathetically in his rocking-chair as the stars put on their performance to honour a truly great performer. I don't suppose he would ever know that he had been so honoured. As I looked down the programme that listed all the performers in this special show, I noticed that the teenager's name was not there – that would have been the ultimate hypocrisy.

Lilian Marsland, from Eccles, Manchester, wrote to me about her favourite picture, though she was sad at heart when she watched it for the first time. Her Grandfather had been a casualty on that historic night in 1912, when the great liner Titanic was lost. There have been many liners lost since the very first liner, the Cunard Britannia, crossed the Atlantic as the first Royal Mail Ship in 1847. The Titanic was a loss caused by man and there have been hundreds of reasons put forward as to why it happened. There are many myths, half-truths and lies about the tragedy including at least three films.

The best picture, giving the most accurate account, was undoubtedly the British film *A Night to Remember*, starring Kenneth Moore and David McCallum. The other two films about the ill-fated liner were *SOS Titanic* and *Titanic*, both American. Neither picture was in the same league as the British movie. Moore played the Second Officer, while McCallum played the heroic Radio Officer. Acclaimed by the Americans, the effects were superb. When they started to make *A Night to Remember* the company had a stroke of luck. The Franconia (a regular visitor to Liverpool and a liner on which I have had the pleasure of working) was partly dismantled, but one complete side of the ship was still intact. It is this side of the Franconia that you see in the part of the film showing the lifeboats descending into the water.

Although I say that the film was fairly accurate, I reserve my opinion on the statements submitted by Captain Lord, from Wallasey and the crew of the Californian. There was a big debate on the timings, the mileage and the SOS signals between the steamer, Californian and the Titanic during the critical two hours after the collision with the iceberg. It should never have hit an iceberg as it was the best equipped ship of its day. Who do you blame? I have got to blame the Titanic's Captain,, Captain Smith. If you have the best ship on the ocean and the best staff and crew and things go wrong, no matter what they may be, the Captain has got to take responsibility. The heavy loss of life however (approximately fifteen hundred passengers) could have been greatly reduced had there been enough lifeboats. The loss of the Titanic, however, brought some positive, long-term benefits as millions of lives have been saved over the past eighty years due to changes in maritime law.

I suppose there has always got to be a first time but it is a pity that it had to be a ship with so many Liverpool and Merseyside connections. Like Mrs Marsland, a great number of Liverpool families suffered that sad night. For them it was not a *Night to Remember* but a night for them to forget.

Stanley Kramer of Columbia Studios calls a halt to another scene as the main actor stumbles forward and holds the back of the upright chair, the knuckles of his hands showing white. The pain is too severe for the sixty seven year old actor, the agony telling on his face and his taut body. He is helped to the couch by his co-stars, Sidney Poitier and Katherine Hepburn. Shooting for the day is cancelled and the studio doctor insists that Mr Tracy needs to rest and must be admitted to hospital. The film *Guess Who's Coming to Dinner* is only halfway through completion and is behind schedule. Scenes which do not involve Tracy have to be brought forward. He is in intensive care and Columbia Pictures hope that the hospital can get him back on his feet as soon as possible.

His co-star in the picture, Katherine Hepburn, has been his friend for over twenty years. They would have married but for the fact that Spencer was against divorcing his wife, Louise Treadwell, whom he had married in 1923. She gave birth to their son John in 1924 but when it was found that he was totally deaf, Louise devoted her life to the cause of the deaf and maintained a high profile as Founder and Director of the John Tracy Clinic for the Deaf and Hard of Hearing. Louise and Spencer remained friends, seeing each other once a week, even though Louise knew of the long and well-publicised affair with Hepburn.

Spencer Tracy, a master actor, was brought up by a drunken father who had hoped that his two children would grow up to be respected in the priesthood. The furthest that either of them got was becoming altar boys. Spencer was a disturbed child and became an unpredictable adult. He was expelled from several schools but the tough Irish kid changed his attitude when he entered a Jesuit-run academy and met Pat O'Brien, who was also to become a great cinema favourite. He encouraged Spencer to go into acting. "Not for me," said Spencer, "it's too effeminate." Spencer was still considering the priesthood when World War I broke out. After being discharged from the Navy, he tried acting and was a success. It was while he was treading the boards that he met an experienced actress, Louise Treadwell.

After Louise gave birth to their son, Spencer had to travel and pressure was put on their marriage. He went to Hollywood but failed several screen tests. Returning to the stage, he was discovered by the famous director, John Lord. Tracy's first film was *Up the River* in 1930, with Humphrey Bogart. Two years and several films later, Katherine Hepburn came into his life at RKO. She won an Oscar in 1933 for her role in *Morning Glory*. When she first met Spencer in the film *Woman of the Year*, Hepburn said to him "I may be a little tall for you, I wear high heels." He replied "Don't worry, I'll cut you down to my size." The two of them were besotted with each other and their affection was so obvious that the studio matched them together in many films. The 1940s became known as the Tracy – Hepburn years, although they were great stars in their own right.

Katherine won Oscars a record four occasions and Spencer was the only actor to win two Oscars in consecutive years with *Captain Courageous* in 1937, and *Boystown*, in which he played a priest, in 1938. Tracy must have gone through turmoil in not fulfilling his father's wishes, although there was one aspect of his life in which he took after his father – drink. Throughout his life his body was ravaged by alcohol abuse, he had his lonely nights, his lost weekends and his benders but he always came back to the film set to give another magnificent performance before returning to the bottle, which helped to ease his troubled conscience. To whom should he turn? Two people loved him and he would have loved to have lived with them both but Louise was devoted to her boy and her work in the clinic. She did, however, play a quiet but active part in Spencer's professional dealings. Spencer had the best of both worlds – two women to help him with his many needs, professionally and affectionately. Then he could return to his other comfort and great love, whether it be Jack Daniels or Johnnie Walker.

Neither his off-screen activities nor his morals had anything to do with his on-screen greatness. He was always big box office and he had millions of fans all over the world. Now he was relying on the hospital staff as they brought him out of intensive care.

The biggest battle of his life was now staged – to finish the picture. He was determined to take his last bow with Katherine. She assisted him through every scene, her eyes glazed as she held back the tears, often with her hand across her face and turning away from the camera. It is worth watching this picture again to witness the gallant performance of these two stars. Fifteen days after the credits were added to the film it was indeed the end for the great Spencer Tracy.

The Greyhound bus pulls into the Los Angeles bus station. "All change" cries the driver. The passengers quickly obey, especially those who are in a hurry to make their connections. Some have to be reminded as they rub their eyes, awakening from a deep sleep. One of these passengers is Johnny Stompanato who is seated at the back of the bus where there is the extra leg room he needs for his giant frame. "All change and that means you at the back."

Johnny staggers to his feet, revealing his height as well over six foot. He stoops as he walks careful not to bang his head. On reaching the front of the bus the colossus looks down at the driver. "Sorry about that, you take your time and watch the step," whimpers the driver, "let me help you with your bag." Johnny Stompanato steps down into the bus station, his presence creating a stir among the other travellers. There are murmers from the women as they stand still and gaze at his impressive physique. This is his first visit to Los Angeles and he looks around arrogantly, as if he owns the place, accepting the flattery from the females with a wry smile. The male travellers look on with envy, feeling inadequate. Johnny moves towards the taxi rank. The former gigolo and bodyguard of gangster Mickey Cohen is going to try his luck in Hollywood.

It will not be long before the ladies of Tinsel Town will be queuing up to sample the prominent endowment which earns Johnny the nickname of Oscar, after the one-foot high academy award statue. His services are sought after by many of the stars of the film colony. It is a wonder that the film studios were not after this handsome masculine frame, because everyone else is! As his reputation grows, he is achieving what he had set out to do – to conquer Hollywood.

After several months of being wined and dined by the famous, he decides to set himself a challenge after reading of the separation of Lana Turner and Lex Barker.

"She must be feeling a bit lonely now and she must have heard of me. Being married to an ex-Tarzan she must like big men and they don't come any better than me." he thinks. He obtains her private phone number through some studio contacts and suggests a blind date, mentioning mutual friends and dropping a hint or two as to why he is nicknamed Oscar.

Lana Turner had had plenty of affairs and marriages. Her romances with Frank Sinatra, Tyrone Power, Fernando Larmus and Howard Hughes had filled the gossip columns for over twenty years. She seemed destined to find violence with her love and her marriages often followed a violent path. Her husbands, though not considered violent men, ended up using Lana as a punch-bag. She was thrown downstairs by one, slapped in a restaurant by another and yet another poured champagne over her in public. Over the years she often had to wear dark glasses to hide her many black eyes. The four husbands involved in these 'Madison Square Garden' events were Artie Shaw, Steve Cane, millionaire playboy Bob Topping and Lex Barker. Which husband did what damage I cannot say but going back over the relationships of her life, Tyrone Power was her only real love and one she lost through her over-possessiveness.

Lana seemed to be attracted towards violence. Now here she was accepting a date with Johnny Stompanato who, as an ex-bodyguard, was no saint. He carried on where the others had left off. Lana told the press "I find men exciting and if any girl says she doesn't, she must be an old maid, a street walker or a saint." She was now obsessed by Johnny but was soon wearing dark glasses again and decided to dispense with his company. After a few more dates, she decided that she could not live without him. Lana was by this time in England filming *Another Time, Another Place* and she wrote steamy letters to him every day.

Lana begged Johnny to come to London and set him up in Millionaire's Row in London. Now he became even more demanding, in fact, he was walking all over her. He threatened "When I say hop, you hop. When I say jump, you jump. If you don't, I will hurt you so much that you will be so repulsive you will have to go into hiding." He walked onto the set of a certain film, pointed a gun at Sean Connery and warned him to stay away or else. The former 007 landed a right hook which floored the big man. The studio informed Scotland Yard and Stompenato was deported from England.

Lana's longing letters continued to arrive at Johnny's home and were as steamy as ever. When her picture was finished, their raunchy affair resumed in Mexico. Johnny had not changed, he was as violent as ever. They returned to North America, where Lana's daughter Cheryl (from her marriage to Steve Crane) waited for them at the airport. Cheryl, who was only fourteen, was concerned for her mother as the press had had a field day over this affair. The three were all at home on Bedford Drive when Cheryl could not take any more of the abuse that her mother was receiving from Johnny and ran into the kitchen, grabbed a pair of scissors and plunged them into Stompenato's stomach, killing him. The police arrived and the customary formalities followed.

Both mother and daughter were questioned. Lana's answers were delivered as she gazed, as if in a trance, at Johnny's body. She knew that this would be the end of her career but what she did not foresee was that all her explicit love letters would end up in the hands of Johnny's former boss, his lifelong friend and gangster, Michael Cohen. He passed them on to the press who filled the front page of their tabloids. It was Cohen's revenge for losing his pal.

The court scenes at the trial were the most dramatic of Lana's career. The jury took only twenty minutes to arrive at a verdict of justifiable homicide. The twelve letters occupied the nations front pages for two days and Lana Turner knew that this was the end. Her mind drifted back to when she looked at Johnny's body being zipped up into the plastic bag, like the final curtain closing for both of them.

The **handsome, teenage immigrant** of no fixed abode was finding it hard on the streets of New York, with only the benches of Central Park to rest on. His mind wandered back to his native Italy. His stomach churned with homesickness when he thought of his childhood and his respectable military family. He got a job as a dishwasher at a restaurant which was part of a dance hall where ladies paid to dance with handsome men and our celebrity was a very handsome, tall and dark.

The soap suds were put aside in favour of a pair of dancing shoes. His dancing ability was only average but he was a quick learner and by watching the other dancing gigolos he soon excelled, especially at the Tango. His stylish rhythm soon got him into the theatre, touring with dancing shows but then he had to move away from New York State because his mistress was charged with the murder of her husband.

Yes, Rudolph Valentino had to move on just as he was making it into the big-time. He joined a dancing troupe and danced his way to San Francisco. He met Norma Carey, the star of *Phantom of the Opera*, who advised him to go to Hollywood because of his Latin looks. Rudy didn't have the fare so he joined another dancing troupe who were heading that way. This was none other than the Al Jolson touring group. Arriving in Hollywood, he was paid five dollars a day and made about fifteen films between 1918 and 1920, mostly typecast as villains and gigolos.

He met film starlet Jean Hacker, fell for her and they married with Rudy not knowing that she had broken off an affair with another actress. The marriage was a disaster and damaged Rudy's macho image. But he need not have worried about his career once he was cast in the leading role in *The Four Horsemen of the Apocalypse*. It required a Latin dancer and was made for this once starving Italian immigrant who was to shorten his name to Rudolph Valentino and become the most sought-after lover in the history of Hollywood. Every studio wanted him, millions of woman desired him and letters poured into Hollywood every week, from all over the world. His five dollars a week had become five hundred dollars. His next film, *The Sheik* doubled his salary again and the hair styles of men changed imitate his sleek, combed-back look. In one film he sported a small beard and all the barbers in America threatened to go on strike in protest, because of the effect it would have on their businesses.

His new wife, Natasha, wanted to direct and choose all his new pictures. Some women were so obsessed with Valentino in his film *Blood and Sand*, where he met his end being gored by the bull, that they committed suicide. Men all over the world were jealous of his tall, dark looks and male press critics raised questions over his manhood. He challenged his critics to fight him in the boxing ring and his great friend, Jack Dempsey, watched as he knocked one reporter out flat. Hollywood had never had a bigger sex symbol but after Natasha left him because of production disputes, he wandered into several affairs.

In 1926 he made the sequel *The Son of the Sheik*. Just before its preview Valentino took ill with appendicitis. Though an operation was successful, peritonitis set in and he went into a coma. He died on 23 August, aged thirty one. No-one's death in the history of America has caused more anguish, pandemonium, riots and suicides than Rudolph Valentino's. He left massive debts and all his possessions had to be sold. What was left was shared between his brother and sister. In his will, he left Natasha just one dollar. His coffin arrived at the cemetery but no plot had been arranged. An old friend opened a family plot to save embarrassment. The studio barons could not provide him with a resting place despite all the millions he had made for them. They were only interested in finding a new Valentino and looked towards Rudolph's brother, Alberto, who had seven operations and plastic surgery on his nose, without success.

To this day, a veiled woman, dressed in black, places flowers at the vault on the 23 August. Perhaps she is a descendant of one of his loved ones?

The young boy looks warily at the swimming pool water in the Chicago Public Baths. It is his first time at the baths. He stands and admires all the other children as they splash about.

"Aren't you going in, son?" asks the attendant.

"Not yet, Sir, I'll … I'll just watch, thank you." Young Peter Donas walks around the pool twice and then a third time. The attendant meets him again.

"Why don't you go under the shower and get the feel of the water. I'll give you a hand at the steps, you'll feel a lot better once you are in." the attendant suggests. "I will stay at the side of the pool." Peter has his shower and descends the steps. The coldness of the water takes his breath away as he clings to the side for dear life, making sure that the attendant is keeping his promise. A boy jumps in, splashing Peter and causing him to gasp for air.

"Are you all right son?" enquires the attendant.

"Y … Y … Yes, I think so." Peter watches the other boys trying to swim. The water feels warmer now and he feels that he could be a little more adventurous and lets go of the side of the pool. He looks up at the attendant and smiles then puts his head under the water, reappearing with a gasp. "That's my boy." the attendant shouts.

Peter Jonas was born in Vienna in 1904, his parents emigrating to America when he was only three. That was five years ago and he is now with his school-mates, splashing water over them and developing his confidence to the full. By his next visit, he is doing the crawl, not only with ease but with speed. No one can believe that this is only his second visit to the baths. He watches the experienced swimmers and is so confident that he thinks that he can do the same. Within two weeks, he has mastered the length of the pool. As the weeks pass, Peter progresses from one length to two lengths to ten lengths. He could swim all day. His speed and style are admired by onlookers. When he needs a bigger challenge he starts to train in Lake Michigan and at the athletic club where his ability is recognised.

At the age of seventeen, he claims his first world record. He glides through the water, the speed and accuracy of his stroke hardly cause a ripple. He delights the crowds as he smashes one record after another, becoming the first man to break the one-minute barrier for the one hundred metres and the five-minute barrier for the five hundred metres. Who could stop this giant of a man? As he dives in, his spectacular strokes bring him to the half-length mark before his competitors have got even a couple of strokes together. At the 1924 Olympics in Paris, at the age of twenty, he climbs on to the winner's rostrum four times. Within the next five years he breaks no less than twenty four world records. Peter Donas looks at his medals and thinks of himself gasping for breath and the attendant smiling at him, giving him a wink and encouragement "Go on, son, you can do it."

By 1929 he needed a new challenge and decided to turn professional and model swim wear. His six-foot three-inch frame, featured on posters and in magazines, caught the eye of Louis B Meyer, of MGM. "We would like you to come to Hollywood, Peter." Meyer invited.

"But I can't act!" was Peter's reply.

"It's quite all right," Meyer continued, "The film does not have a big speaking part, women just love your frame in those swimming briefs. But this time it will be a loin-cloth."

Yes, Peter Donas, was to become Johnny Weissmuller, star of *Tarzan of the Apes*. The film was a big hit and MGM could not wait to get Johnny swinging through the trees again, giving his Austrian yell mixed with a gorilla cry! His swimming and diving were excellent as this is what he did best. Most of the stunts were done by Johnny, especially with the dummy crocodiles and the tame lions, but it was all made to look real. He made twelve films in total. Jane, his jungle partner, was portrayed by Maureen O'Sullivan, mother of Mia Farrow with Boy played by Johnny Sheffield. My favourite of the Tarzan series was *Tarzan's New York Adventures* where he actually dives off Brooklyn Bridge. The partnership of this jungle trio certainly swelled the bank balance of the author, Edgar

Rice Burrows, who wrote twenty five books about the hero. They were translated into thirty languages and were also featured on radio and in comic strips.

There have been many film Tarzans. I remember Bruce Bennett (whose real name was Herman Brix) who relinquished the title to Johnny. Lex Barker came after him and then there was Gordon Scott, but none of them came even close to the great Johnny Weissmuller. He had all the attributes of a great athlete and had the medals to prove it.

When the time came for Johnny to hang up his loin-cloth, he moved from MGM to Columbia to carry on his wild adventures as Jungle Jim. This time Johnny kept his clothes on and his popularity soared when Jungle Jim transferred to television. He subsequently had to retire from active life due to heart disease. He got weaker and weaker but was persuaded to play host to the millions who passed through Las Vegas at Caesar's Palace. Customers liked to shake his hand and have their photographs taken with him. Joe Louis did the same when nearing the end of his life. Johnny's heart condition was followed by a stroke which made him housebound.

He sits in a wheelchair and reflects on his athletic life that spanned from his gasps for breath as he made his first dip in the pool to his plunge off Brooklyn Bridge. From his swimming strokes which made him famous to the stroke that now renders him helpless. Still, there is a new attendant now who moves Johnny's chair so that he can see the sunset. Johnny died on the 20 January 1984.

"**Ladies and gentlemen** – we interrupt our programme to bring you a special bulletin. At twenty minutes before eight this evening, Professor Farrall of Mount Jenning Observatory reported several explosions of incandescent gas on the planet Mars. The spectrograph indicates the gas to be hydrogen and moving towards Earth." These are the words Orson Welles spoke as he interrupted the radio music of La Compasita on the American radio station on 8 October 1938. The sudden shock of this interruption had cars and taxis pulling into the side of the road – while others crashed into each other as pedestrians ran in panic, to either phone home or the radio station.

The city streets of Eastern America were pandemonium. People were screaming and others crying after hearing "We are being invaded, the Martians are coming!" Radios blared out from bars which were becoming increasingly busy and drink was being consumed as if there was no tomorrow. Or was there?

The broadcast continued and, after some music, came the announcement "We interrupt your music to give you an update of the information previously given from Mount Jennings Observatory. A huge flaming object, believed to be a meteorite had landed near Trenton, close to New Jersey. We shall now carry on with some more music, we shall return to Mount Jennings as soon as we get any further details. In the meantime, we continue with Tommy Dorsey and his Orchestra." Within a few seconds, the band is interrupted again by the announcer. "We take you to a reporter at the scene in New Jersey." The reporter breathlessly cries out "Good heavens, something is wriggling out of the shadows like a snake ... now there is another, and another ... there, I can see the thing's body, it's as large as a bear and it glistens like wet leather, but that face ... it is incredible! I can hardly bear to look at it, it is like a serpent with black, jet-black eyes, its mouth is like a ... in fact it is V-shaped and dripping with saliva from rimless lips which are quivering and pulsating ..." A scream is heard amongst the crackling of the radio which now goes dead but comes alive again with the voice of the radio announcer "We now return to some more music."

Cities were gripped in a state of terror. The radio programme continued with Orson Welles describing the battle with the Martians and the death and destruction it had caused. Millions of Americans remained glued to their radios, completely terrified, unable to contact their loved ones. What was there to do but listen and hope for some good news. Those who were not listening to the radio were in the churches, synagogues, or gospel halls. Orson Welles reached the climax of the story and then, with tongue in cheek, added "If your doorbell rings tonight and there is nobody there, that was no Martian, this is Halloween."

So realistic was the broadcast that the Americans really thought they were being invaded with very few realising that it was a hoax. One day only a few people at the radio station knew of Orson Welles, the next day three quarters of the world knew of this twenty three year old. Hollywood greeted him but at arms length as they were afraid of him. He was so bright as a child that at two years of age his bedtime stories were tales from Shakespeare. At three he was reading Shakespeare himself and, by the age of seven, he knew King Lear by heart. By the age of ten, he had learned all the great tragic roles. When he had been in Hollywood for three years, he formed a company actors, including Joseph Cotton.

His film *Citizen Kane* is considered a masterpiece of cinema He co-wrote the script, produced, directed and starred in it. He also introduced low camera angles and special lighting well in advance of any film produced at that time. A year later he directed *The Magnificent Ambersons* for RKO. During its production, RKO was sold into new ownership and the film was cut by a third. The end result was that Orson Welles was fired.

Welles' marriage to Rita Heyworth was billed by the media as Beauty and the Brain. It was to last five years, with Rita saying "I couldn't stand his genius anymore."

My memories of Orson Welles are associated with the haunting theme of Harry Lime, a role he played in *The Third Man* in 1949. Lying in the archives are many Orson Welles productions, films which were made but never released. The Hollywood moguls thought that the public were not yet ready for such movies but, in my opinion, had those films been released, they would have made Orson Welles even more powerful. It was sad to see this very talented man reduced to advertising sherry.

He died of a heart attack in 1985, at the age of seventy. Orson Welles was not the Third Man – he was Number One.

"**Can you walk across the street,** drop your ice-cream and then start crying?" Director Irving Pitchler asks the four year old girl with the big, dark eyes and lovable features.

"Of course she can." replies the little girl's mother, "my little Natasha can do anything you ask." The mother, Marie Gurdin, of Russian descent, is hell-bent on getting her little girl into films and on this day in San Francisco in 1942, when she hears that a movie was being made, she takes her daughter to the film set. Little Natasha is perfect and cries so naturally that the director promised to send for her at a later date for more work.

Two years later, Irving Pitchler had not forgotten those big, dark eyes and Natasha Gurdin was to become one of the most sought-after actresses in Hollywood. By taking the first three letters of Natasha and then using the last four letters of the film capital, her name was changed to Natalie Wood.

It had not been an easy life for Natalie as she was dragged from one film set to another by a mother determined to make her a star. She disregarded Natalie's emotional state and in order to get a scene right, she would tell her horrific stories to terrify her. She would then return to the set with Natalie and inform the director "She's all yours now!" In 1949, during the making of the film *Green Promise*, Natalie's mother may have caused her to develop what was to be a lifelong fear of water. Natalie had to cross a small wooden bridge in a torrential rainstorm. Marie Gurdin told Natalie that it was safe to cross but she lied as the bridge had been rigged to collapse in order to make it more authentic. Natalie was thrown into the water and feared for her life. Life guards were standing by but Natalie was totally unaware of this.

This is how child stars were treated in Hollywood. What made it worse was that her own mother was behind the manipulation. When Natalie was old enough to realise what had been going on she was very angry and promised that nothing like that would ever happen to her own children.

As an adult star she had a magnetic personality and many male stars sought her affections. Anyone who played opposite her fell in love with her and she with them – including James Dean and Warren Beatty. Raymond Burr (Perry Mason) said that he would leave films altogether in order to be with her. She was linked with many stars but there were some that she wasn't keen on. One in particular was Elvis Presley. She said that when she was with Elvis she felt old-fashioned and that he was a real 'mummy's boy'. They also had no privacy. If they went to a movie Elvis had to hire the cinema for a private showing and would be surrounded by bodyguards. She recalled "I made a phone call to the studios to get them to ring back and say I was needed on set just to get away."

Natalie made it as a child star as well as an adult. While a child star she had played the daughter of all the top stars, including Bing Crosby in *Just For You* in 1952 and Maureen O'Hara in *Miracle on 34th Street*. As an adult, her biggest breakthrough was as Maria in *West Side Story*. She made this spectacular following her successful role with James Dean in *Rebel Without a Cause*, much against her family's wishes. "Who cares?" was her attitude after all the things her mother had put her through on the road to stardom.

Splendour in the Grass with Warren Beatty gave the press a field day over their affair but, after this, came the real love of her life, Robert Wagner. They married in 1957, but the marriage only lasted six years, which I suppose is pretty good going by Hollywood standards.

After the divorce, Natalie was alone and depressed. As the depression took its toll she switched herself off from all productions, staying at home and cutting off even her closest friends. She longed for male company and hoped that some day she would be happily married and have children. She would give up the Hollywood stardom just to settle down to married life. Still she stayed at home, her depression getting deeper and deeper until she decided to end her life by an overdose of sleeping pills. She was saved at the brink of death by the determination of a friend, Martin Crowle, who constantly stayed in touch with her. He brought her out of her shell, with the hope that she may meet someone and that she could be happy again.

Once back in the limelight, Natalie fell into the arms of film producer Richard Gregson. They married, had a little girl called Natasha and appeared to be very happy until Natalie overheard a phone conversation between Gregson and his secretary! Divorce followed. This was a terrible blow to Natalie, who had been working hard to make a happy marriage. She doted on her little girl Natasha and hoped that it would not be too long before her dream of settling down was complete. But alas, the depression set in once more. Martin Crowle came again to her rescue and whisked her away on a cruise.

She came back rejuvenated, making more successful films as well as catching the eye once more of her first and possibly only love, Robert Wagner. They married again and Natalie gave birth to a little girl named Courtney. Natalie's dream now seemed complete, she was apparently deeply in love and had two lovely girls. The family enjoyed life to the full and she had every luxury Hollywood could provide, including a yacht to take them to coastal resorts in the breaks from filming. They were taking one of these breaks, from the film *Brainstorm* in 1983 with co-star Christopher Walker. He and Robert were said to have been quarrelling on board the yacht when Natalie (who, as I explained earlier, had been terrified of water since she was a child) went missing. She was found drowned off Cantalina Island hours later, with a very high blood alcohol level. There was a great deal of speculation at the time – two men quarrelling, her history of depression and her past suicide attempt. The title of the film that she was appearing in at the time, *Brainstorm*, seems apt as the curtains close at the end of another Hollywood mystery.